CLAN TEXAS

MARIAN CUMMING

Illustrated by Peter Burchard

HARCOURT, BRACE AND COMPANY

NEW YORK

With love to
Winifred Fairbrother
and
Helen Browne
Two English Women
with Texas deep in their hearts

CLAN TEXAS

· ONE ·

MR. ADAMS, the teacher, pulled out his big gold-cased watch, snapped it open, looked at it, snapped it shut, then smoothed down his curly brown beard. The children watched him eagerly. Was it time?

"Put away your books and face the room," said Mr. Adams. "Please get out your compositions for the contest." A rustle went through the little one-room school on the Texas prairie. Books were closed and piled neatly on the shelf that extended around three walls of the room and that served as desk for all the pupils. Thirty-seven boys and girls, who had been facing the shelf, swung their legs over the bench and faced into the room and toward the teacher. The girls smoothed their curls or braids and adjusted their gingham skirts; the boys gave a lick to their hair and twisted their bare feet under the bench. Each held a folded paper. This was an important moment.

Karl Zorn, on the bench opposite the door, pushed his straight blond hair out of his eyes and clutched his composition tightly. He had worked hard on it. He hoped it would take the prize. Early in the term

Mr. Adams had said that he would give three lead pencils to the pupil who wrote the best composition on his favorite hero. This was a prize worth working for; pencils were scarce and expensive in Texas in 1873. The children used slates and slate pencils, or, if they wrote on paper, used charred cypress twigs. Karl had copied his composition at home on foolscap with Pa's lead pencil, so he knew it looked neat. He hoped that would help in the judging when Mr. Adams read it. He was anxious to hand it in.

Each boy and girl had chosen a hero to write about. Karl didn't think anyone else would have selected his hero. He had chosen to tell about Dr. Brenham, for whom the little town of Brenham, just down the road about three miles, was named. It was a neat, quiet little town with many German settlers. There Karl's father did his trading and there they all went to church on Sunday. Karl didn't think many people knew about the man it had been named for. He had talked to some of the old-timers who had known the brave doctor.

To his dismay now he heard Mr. Adams say, "Each pupil will read his own composition aloud. We will begin with Ramon Ruiz here in front."

As Ramon began to read in his soft voice, Karl sat appalled. To read your composition aloud before the whole school! Writing his composition had been fun but to read it aloud was different. The reading started on the other side of the room. It would be a while before his turn came. But already Karl's cheeks began to burn and his hands were wet.

He was as hot as though it were summertime, but this was only May—almost time for school to end. A cool breeze from the far-away Gulf was coming through the door and the two rough windows. It was nice to have the windows open, Karl thought. In winter when it was cold or rainy they were closed and as they had no glass panes, only wooden shutters, that made the room dark and stuffy. But now the breeze was sweeping in. No reason to feel so hot and choking.

Karl looked at the other children to see if they seemed as nervous as he was. They were sitting erect on the benches, listening and waiting for their turn. He couldn't tell how they were feeling. Karl hoped they couldn't see how scared he was. Bill Riley, the biggest boy in school, sat slumped on the bench, his big bare feet sticking out before him. Everything about Bill was big—his hands, his feet, his shock of thick black hair and eyebrows, his heavy shoulders and his voice. Bill didn't look afraid.

Karl wondered who Bill's hero was. Bill was a sort of hero himself. He could out-fight anyone in school. When they walked barefooted in the grass-burs, Bill always could walk the farthest. Karl half-admired him and half-feared him. He admired him because

Bill was everything Karl was not. Bill was big and strong and bold; Karl was small and timid. He was afraid of him because Bill teased and pestered the small boys who couldn't fight back. Next to Bill sat Tom Carr, who followed Bill like his shadow and tried to be just like him. Tom was now copying Bill's careless slouch as they listened.

Most of the compositions were about people they had studied in school: General Lee, Sam Houston, Travis at the Alamo. There wasn't much that Karl hadn't heard again and again. Katy Riley, Bill's sister, told about Jane Long, "the mother of Texas." Tom Carr told about George Washington. His composition was very short.

At last Mr. Adams came to Bill. The big boy rose slowly to his feet. His hero hadn't been in any history book. A few months before, the little town of Brenham had been shocked by the arrest and escape of a noted cattle rustler. There had been a fight, several men wounded. Bill chose to tell about the life of the outlaw and his exploits and his final escape. He made it sound exciting. Karl thought, "Bill will surely get the prize." Mr. Adams only said, "Thank you, Bill. Next."

The reading went on and Karl wiped his hands on his pant legs. His breath came fast. It wouldn't be long before his turn now.

Just then he happened to look out the door. There

were Ma and Pa coming across the schoolyard! What on earth were they doing at school? They stopped at the doorstep, looking into the schoolroom.

"May we come in, Mr. Adams?" came Pa's deep, slow voice. "Mrs. Zorn and I are on the way home from Brenham and we thought we could give Karl and any of the others going our way a ride home."

"Come in, come in," said Mr. Adams cordially. Mr. Zorn was one of the men who had helped start this little school and he paid part of Mr. Adams' salary. "I am sure you will not mind waiting. The pupils are reading their compositions in our prize contest. I think you will enjoy hearing them. Karl has not read yet so you will get to hear him."

Karl listened in dismay. Having Pa and Ma as audience was the last straw! Ma had heard him read his composition again and again and Pa had helped him get some of the facts for it, but it was quite different, reading before them as well as the whole school.

Even so they did look nice, sitting on the bench up by the teacher's desk, and Karl was proud of them. Pa had on his town clothes and sat with his wide hat in his lap. He was big and bearded and solid. Ma was little and trim. She never wore a sunbonnet away from home. She had on a blue cotton dress and a little black "dress bonnet." Her soft blond hair, that was so much like Karl's, was smooth in front, and below the bonnet in back it was braided in a big

7

knot. Her blue eyes smiled lovingly just once at Karl and then she looked at the wall above him. Ma always knew how he felt.

When Karl got up to read Ma watched him proudly. His fair face was flushed. His hands that held the paper trembled. "Bless the kindchen," thought Ma. "This is going to be hard for him. But you can do it, Karl dear, you can do it."

Karl began in a little voice. "My hero was a very brave man and we ought to know all about him. He came from near here and his name was Dr. Richard Fox Brenham." There was a little stir in the room. No one knew anything about Dr. Brenham and Karl had caught their interest. He went on, encouraged. "He was a good doctor. He took good care of his patients. He would go to them whenever they wanted him, no matter how bad the weather. A lot of old people here remember his kindness and gentleness."

The children looked disappointed. Was Karl just going to tell about a country doctor? Karl went on. "But he was not just a good doctor. He was a fighter and very heroic." Karl was now so interested in what he was reading that his paper steadied in his hands.

Dr. Brenham had been in the Texas army and had gone on many expeditions when he was needed. The Mier expedition was one of them. It had gone down to protect the border between Texas and Mexico. The men were all captured by Mexican soldiers and put in prison, at Salado.

"There was just one narrow door guarded by a soldier with a bayonet," read Karl carefully. He was so interested in his story now that he wasn't thinking about anything else. "The Texans did not have any weapons but they wanted to escape. The first man out the narrow door certainly would be killed but the others might have a chance. Dr. Brenham said that he had no wife or children at home waiting for him so he would go first. So he did and he was killed. The rest escaped but they were captured later. The city of Brenham is named for my hero, Dr. Brenham."

Karl waited a minute and then sat down. "Whew! That's over!" he thought. He looked at Pa and Ma. They smiled at him proudly.

Mr. Adams rose slowly. "You have all done good work," he said. "You have studied and given real reasons for your choices of heroes. Bill and Karl have done original research and not just depended on what they could find in books. I like that. And I like having heroes from our own part of the country. But Bill's hero, while he showed bravery, was only fighting to save his skin. He was an outlaw. He is not a hero that I would like you to copy. Dr. Brenham

9

fought for freedom and gave his life for his fellow prisoners. Karl has told his story well. I am awarding the prize to Karl Zorn."

He held out the package with the pencils in it and Karl came forward. Everybody clapped. Bill rose and shouted, "That's not fair. My hero did what he started out to do and escaped. Karl's was killed and the prisoners were captured again. It wasn't any *use*."

"Sit down, Bill," said Mr. Adams sternly. "The decision is made. As you grow up you will learn what real bravery is. Now, school is dismissed."

Karl went out with the other children, while Pa and Ma stayed inside to talk to Mr. Adams. The children gathered around Karl and looked at the nice

pencils. "They are better than burnt cypress twigs," said one. "Or slates and slate pencils," said another.

Bill and Tom stood at one side. Karl could tell Bill was still mad. He looked at Karl in the midst of the children. "Little sissy," he drawled. "Teacher's pet! Dr. Brenham was just a softy, like you! Couldn't do anything!"

"He could! He did! He died! Nobody could do any more than die to save the others," Karl protested. It wasn't so bad if Bill said things about him, but Karl couldn't let his hero be abused.

"Aw, shut up, Miss Carlotta!" Bill said. "If my Ma and Pa had been here I'd'a' had the prize. Showing off!"

"Old show-off!" echoed Tom, agreeing, as always, with Bill.

Bill turned on him. "You and your composition out of the book!" he sneered. "You *all* make me sick! I'm going home."

Pa and Ma came out of the school. "Who's going my way?" called Pa. "Bill? Katy? Tom? Room for you all."

Katy and Tom started with Karl toward the wagon. "I'll walk," said Bill curtly. Bill was very mad, Karl thought, to walk three miles or more, rather than ride with them.

He was glad school was almost over. He would be glad not to see Bill for a while. Then he thought that after school closed he wouldn't see much of the other children until fall and he wasn't so glad. Summer on the farm was a busy time and there wasn't much chance to go visiting. And except for the Rileys and the Peters everyone lived too far away. Vacation was fun but it was lonely on the farm.

· TWO ·

[The summer passed as quietly as Karl had thought
it would. He spent many days working in the fields
with Pa and other afternoons lazing in the slat ham-
mock under the trees at the side of the house with a
book. Once Pee Wee Peters, Karl's nearest neighbor,
came over and fished with him down at the creek.
Then Pee Wee went to Austin to visit his grandmother and there was no one to do anything with,
for Karl didn't count the Rileys.

Each Sunday there was the trip to Brenham for
services, and sometimes Karl drove to town with Pa
for supplies. But the trip was hot and sunny. Ma said
it was enough to boil his brains, and Karl often stayed
at home in the shade instead.

So Karl was glad when camp meeting time came,
as it did every year in August, and the Zorns, with all
the other families living around Brenham, went to
camp for two weeks on the banks of Jordan Creek.
It was fun to pack up their things and leave the farm
and go in the wagon to the camp grounds, and it was

fun living in one of the tents grouped around the brush-covered tabernacle and eating outside.

Most of all Karl enjoyed seeing all the people and his schoolmates and the teacher. It was good to be in a crowd. People had come from all over central Texas to this meeting. They had come in buggies and wagons and on horseback and each family lived in a tent or rough shack. Some of the people, whose homes were nearby, came just for the day and ate their lunch picnic fashion and attended the three daily meetings. But most of them came and stayed the whole two weeks.

The meetings were exciting and noisy. Brother Richards, the preacher, had a big commanding voice and he could really lash out at the sinners. In no time at all he had the whole congregation shouting and saying "Amen!" and coming up in droves to the mourner's bench. He led the singing, too, without the help of an organ—fine lusty hymns with excitement and rhythm: *When the First Trumpet Sounds, On Canaan's Happy Shore* and *Stand up, Stand up for Jesus.* Karl had sung himself hoarse.

But that had been two weeks ago and there had been three meetings a day every one of those fourteen days. Now it was the last day and Karl, sitting between Ma and Pa on the hard bench, was plumb tired of it all. The shouting and the hymns were old to him now. They just sounded noisy. The constant crowds had made the dust hang heavy in the tabernacle and the August morning was hot. Big palm leaf fans waved in a sleepy rhythm. Most of the sinners had come up and "professed" now so there wasn't the excitement there had been at first.

Karl looked at Ma, sitting beside him. Her face was lifted and her blue eyes were shining. Ma loved camp meeting. She was a quiet person so she wasn't a shouter, but she gave a fervent "Praise the Lord!" when she agreed with the preacher, and she sang all the hymns in her clear sweet voice. *She* wasn't a bit tired of camp meeting.

Karl stole a look at Pa, on the other side of him. He couldn't tell how he was feeling. Pa's beard hid part of his expression and his eyes were fixed on the preacher. But Karl noticed that his fingers were beating a silent tattoo on the brim of his hat. Was Pa tired of camp meeting too?

If he was, he did something about it. After lunch he rose from the table and said, "You go on to meeting. I have to go down to the shed and see about the team if we are to drive home after the afternoon meeting."

Ma sniffed. "Ach, you just want to go talk with the men who stay away from meeting and hang around the sheds."

Pa smiled. "Well, Lena, talk is good, too. Not

often do I get a chance like this," and he swung down the dusty lane that led toward the sheds.

(Karl wondered if he could get out of it as easily. He helped Ma clear up after lunch and washed his face and slicked down his hair. Then he said, all in a rush, "Ma, can I go over with Pa to the wagon shed instead of meeting? Can I, Ma, can I?" He waited uneasily. Would Ma think he was backsliding?

Ma was putting on her dress bonnet, tying the strings under her chin as she looked in the mirror hanging on the pole of the tent. Even in camp Ma was as spandy clean as she was at home. The tent was kept spotless and she didn't wear calico and sunbonnets to meeting like some of the women. Her cool white lawn dress was stiffly starched and smelled of soap and sunshine. Her face was peaceful and up-lifted looking, thinking of the meeting to come.

She smiled at Karl, standing so stiff and anxious. "It's the last day, Karlchen," she reminded him. "And it will be a whole year before we have another. Don't you *want* to go?"

"But so many meetings there are!" he said. "They are nice but I'd like to go with Pa." He waited.

"Menfolks!" sighed Ma. The meetings that were so tiresome to Karl were a deep source of joy to her. After months on a Texas farm it was inspiring to hear the voices of her friends and neighbors raised in

16

prayer and praise. The two weeks had gone much too quickly for her.

But for a little boy it was different. "Go along with Pa," she said. "Come back when you hear us singing, *God be with you till we meet again.* That always winds up the last meeting."

She smoothed down his hair and put his battered straw hat on it. "You'll have to have a new hat for school," she said. "Summer's almost over."

Summer was very much present, however, as Karl stepped from the shadow of the live-oak trees around the tents into the dusty road that led to the wagon sheds. It was still and hot. The sun that was opening the cotton on the Zorn farm was beating down on the camp grounds. It beat upon the tabernacle with its roof of boughs and open sides. As Karl skirted it he could hear the choir tuning up and the murmur of many voices, with Brother Richard booming out greetings above them all. That man sure had a mighty voice!

Ma hoped Karl would be a preacher when he grew up but Karl wanted to be a doctor—maybe like brave Dr. Brenham. Karl thought of his hero's life and death. Suddenly Karl was not a little tow-headed German-American boy in clean jeans and a torn straw hat. *He* was the handsome soldier-surgeon, "tall and of commanding physique," leading his fellow prisoners to freedom. He felt the fear and uncertainty inside the jail; he imagined the Mexican guard with his bayonet fixed. "I have no wife and children," murmured Karl and all unarmed he led the men forward. He fell with the enemy's bayonet in his brave heart just as he came out into a clearing by the creek.

"What's the matter, baby? Can't you walk?"

Karl scrambled to his feet. He saw Bill Riley, swinging alone on a grapevine swing.

"Stumbled," muttered Karl. He didn't want Bill to know he had been pretending. Bill would be sure to tease him.

"You get out of meeting, too? Come on and swing," invited Bill. Karl was flattered at the unexpected invitation but he would rather be with Bill when the other boys were around. He didn't trust Bill.

"Can't now," he said importantly to hide his timidity. "Going over to the wagons with the men."

He watched a minute as Bill swung higher and higher. It was wonderful how Bill kept his big wide-brimmed hat on when he was almost upside down. Karl thought, "Maybe my folks will get me a real hat instead of an old straw one or just a cap for school." It would be easier pretending to be a Texas hero if he had a big Texas hat. Easier to be a brave boy, too.

He walked along the banks of Jordan Creek, so much clearer than the muddy Brazos into which it flowed. Here was the place where they got their drinking water and here was the small green tree that had been kept burning slowly, so that if anyone's fire went out he could always get a fresh light. It gave off a pungent, musty smell. Farther down was the pool where the men and boys went swimming and below that, the horses' watering place, all muddy and roiled with their tracks.

Near this were the wagon sheds and the pasture. Karl heard the horses and the men's voices. The men were by the sheds, some sitting on the fence, some on boxes or on wagon seats set on the grass, some just squatting down against the wall of a shed. Pa was sitting on a wagon seat with another man that Karl didn't know. Karl saw Mr. Adams on a box nearby and recognized the doctor and the mayor by their tall Bee-Gum hats.

"Ma say you could come?" asked Pa as Karl joined him. Karl nodded. Pa squeezed his big body into a smaller space so Karl could sit between him and the strange young man.

"This is my son Karl, Mr. Cartwright," said Pa. "Mr. Cartwright has come out from England, Karl. He was telling us about his work."

Karl looked shyly at Mr. Cartwright. He was different from the other men. He wore a dark suit and a smallish dark hat, instead of the easy trousers and

shirts and big hats of most of the Texans. And while
they lounged with their hands in their pockets or
slouched against the fence, Mr. Cartwright sat with
his body erect and his shoulders back, like a soldier.
His hair was curly and blond and his sideburns
glistened in the sunshine. He gave Karl a quick smile.

"Karl will not be interested, but I think you men
will," he said in his clear clipped voice. "I am helping English immigrants to come to Texas. If you need
laborers, you advance the money for their passage.
They will work for you until it is paid out."

"How do we know they will?" said the mayor.
"You can't indenture a man in Texas. You can't
hold him for the debt."

"That is true," said Mr. Cartwright. "But, gentlemen, these people are penniless. Think what a new start means to them! A few months working out their passage is a small price to pay."

"What is the arrangement?" asked Pa in his slow considering voice. "How do you come into it?"

"I take orders for immigrants from you and am paid so much for each order. My cousin, Joseph McBride, is in London, collecting the immigrants."

"Can they get here in time for the cotton crop?" someone asked.

"I am expecting the first ship, the *Mississippi,* in September," said Mr. Cartwright. "There will be more later if these work out well and there are more orders."

"It sounds like a good thing," said Mr. Adams.

Pa said slowly, "I'd like to have a man and his grown son for my place. And the wife could help Ma in the house. Aunt Narcisse is getting old and wants to go to her daughter. The two boys I have as field hands are going to Houston to work. I think I will put in an order."

Karl had been listening hard. "Can you order people?" he asked. It sounded very strange.

"Yes, lad," smiled Mr. Cartwright. "Do you need some field hands?"

"No," said Karl seriously, "but I'd like a boy just my age." He was sorry he had said it when all the

men broke into a roar of laughter. But he meant it.
There were no children near the farm. During school
term it was not so bad but vacations were lonely. It
would have been nice to have a boy with him all the
time and on the long walk back and forth from
school.

Still laughing, the men broke up into small groups.
Some of them were talking politics—about the mess
in the government at Austin and some of the doings
of the Fire Brigade. Others were just swapping
stories and the news of crops. They enjoyed being
together.

Karl sat by Pa and watched them and thought
about hats. Mr. Cartwright's was dark and small and
different. The professional men of the town wore
high silk Bee-Gum hats—you could have put a hive
of bees in them, like the bee-gum trees. But all the
outdoor men—the farmers, the ranchmen, the sheriff
—and the young men wore wide-brimmed hats. Each
man wore his hat in his own way—straight across his
forehead like Pa, or pushed back on his head like the
young men, or rolled in the brim, or dipped down in
front or cocked on one side. Some were straw and
some were felt but they all looked jaunty and ready
for action. Karl thought of Bill's big hat. He was
sure he was old enough for a big one too.

He was about to say this to Pa when they heard
the strains of *God be with you till we meet again*

from the meeting and the group broke up. The men went toward the tents to start the business of packing and getting home before dark. Karl and Pa walked toward their tent.

"Pa," said Karl. "Do you think I could have a big western hat when I get my school clothes?"

"We'll see, my son, we'll see. Cotton crop is not in yet. But if all goes well I think maybe you can." Pa chuckled deep as he thought of Karl's other request. "Which do you want the most, a boy or a big hat?"

"A big hat," said Karl with decision. He knew there was no chance of getting a boy.

· THREE ·

PA SEEMED HAPPY. He slapped the reins on the team and hummed an old German song. Karl, on the wagon seat beside him, sang silently along with him. But instead of "Ach, du lieber Augustine" he was singing in his mind, "Going to get a big, brave hat, big brave hat. Going to get a big brave hat, get a big hat."

The hat had been in Karl's mind ever since camp meeting three weeks ago. He had tired Ma and Pa out, talking about it. What he wanted was not an old ten cent straw field hat—everyone wore those—but a *big* wide-brimmed hat, the kind the men and big boys wore.

Karl and Pa were on their way from the farm to Brenham to buy school supplies and clothes for school—jean for Ma to make into trousers and gingham for blouses—and the hat. The cotton crop was in and paid for. The Zorn family had money to spend.

It was a happy day, a golden day. The long dry summer had left the Texas fields tinged with yellow and all the autumn flowers were yellow, too—a mist of tiny golden blossoms over the fields and a froth of big yellow daisies and sunflowers and goldenrod along the fences and roadside. The cane and willows in the hollows between the hills were greeny-yellow. The ripe chinaberries hung like golden ornaments on the trees.

The morning sunshine poured over all, over the autumn fields and woods and over Pa's tanned face and brown beard, on Karl's neatly combed hair and happy face and even on his bare feet propped on the dashboard.

"My new hat," said Karl, looking up at Pa. "Could we buy that first of all, please, I *need* that hat." This, he felt, was the real reason for the trip.

"Well, not first," said Pa slowly, and he smiled down at the eager face beside him. Pa always spoke slowly. Generally he spoke slow and easy and amused, as now, but sometimes he spoke slow and deep and stern and at those times Karl knew there was no argument. Pa was boss. Now he said, "First, we stop at Mr. Cartwright's house on this side of town. You must sit still while we talk business."

"Yes, sir," said Karl. "Then we'll get the hat. A nice *big* sombrero? Not another cap or little old straw."

"Well, a boy-size big hat," Pa amended. "I will see how much they cost. Maybe a small big hat wouldn't be too much."

"Like the big boys wear," Karl urged. "And the

sheriff, and the cowboys and the Mexicans. And like *you* wear," with a side glance at Pa's wide sheltering brim. Pa smiled again. He was in a good humor. Karl thought there was a good chance Pa would buy that hat.

"Seems like all the big brave men wear big hats. Bill wears one." Karl added that as if that clinched it.

"Bill's no big brave man," said Pa. Then he said, "I want to see Mr. Cartwright about that family I ordered for our place."

"I still think it sounds funny to order people," said Karl.

"A good thing, in this case," Pa said. "These people would not be able to come to this new land unless there was some sort of arrangement like this. And people here want good steady workers."

Karl liked it when Pa talked to him like he was grown-up. "It must be pretty hard for them to leave their homes and come way out to Texas." Karl loved his home; the idea of going to a strange new place was frightening.

"Well do I know that," said Pa. "But that is the way a new country like this is settled. Why, Karlchen, did you not know I was an immigrant once?"

"Were you *ordered?*" asked Karl. The idea of anyone ordering his big masterful father, like a sack of flour, was disturbing.

"No, I was lucky. I had money enough for my passage and a thousand dollars hidden in my belt, enough to buy my land here. But I came all alone from Germany and I couldn't speak a word of English. That was in '57, sixteen years ago."

Sixteen years, thought Karl, and now Pa had a good farm and was as American as anyone. And in a little while these immigrants would be American too. He stopped feeling sorry for them. Another idea struck him.

"Was Ma an immigrant?" he asked.

"Yes," said Pa. "I had courted her in the old country and when I had my farm well started I sent for her. She came by ship to Galveston and we were married there. What a pretty bride she was, my little Lena!"

"She is pretty now," said Karl.

They were coming into Brenham now. The road had been winding through the softly rolling hills and they could see the cluster of neatly painted houses with the courthouse and stores in the center. They drew up at Mrs. Heine's little house where Mr. Cartwright had his room and office. Karl liked Mr. Cartwright even if he did talk funny and call Karl "lad."

Mr. Cartwright met them at the door. "Come in," he said. "I have something to show you. Bring the lad."

They went into the little office that opened out of Mr. Cartwright's bedroom. The door between was open and Karl saw that both rooms were piled with all sorts of things, dress goods and books and guns and boxes full of other things. In the front room was a large portrait of Queen Victoria and over Mr. Cartwright's bed was a picture of a lot of people all dressed up. Mr. Cartwright saw Karl looking at it.

"That is my family in England," he said proudly. "That little fellow is my brother Charley. He is about your age, Karl, but he is a frail lad. I wrote him that if I had him here he could learn to ride horses and rope bullocks."

"He means steers!" thought Karl. He wandered around looking at all the things.

"My people sent these out for me to sell here," said Mr. Cartwright. "It's a terrible bother. I'm no linen-draper. I don't think they realize how civilized Texas is."

"Beads and red flannel for the natives," chuckled Pa.

"Exactly," laughed Mr. Cartwright. "Look around all you want, lad. Then when your father and I finish our business I'll show everything to you."

There wasn't much that was interesting to see, Karl decided; just like a general store. The guns looked exciting but Karl knew better than to touch them. The books were grown-up books that he couldn't read and the dry-goods and ribbons were women's stuff.

In a box on a chair were some things that Karl couldn't make out. They were like flat oblong purses or bags, dark blue or green or plaid. Ribbons bound the edges and hung down in streamers from one end. They were very puzzling. He soon got tired looking and came and sat on the edge of a chair and listened to Mr. Cartwright's crisp voice.

"I know the ship is late. A lot of people have complained about it because they were counting on help for the fall crops. They must have run into bad weather. It is hard for everyone. I won't get paid for my part until the workers come. That is one reason why I am glad to make a little on the haberdashery."

"Bad, bad," said Pa. "My crops are in, but I wanted to know just what I was getting so I could be ready for them."

"I have a good family down for you, the Gordons, Scottish people. Father and son to work on the farm and the mother to help in the house. That was what you wanted, wasn't it?"

"Fine," said Pa. "They can live in the little cabin that was the first building on the farm. They will eat with us, of course. I will be glad to see them. Now what about this store-keeping of yours?"

They started to look at all the things on the chairs and table and bed. First Pa looked at the woolen cloth and shook his head. "It will not sell. Too hot for this climate. Texas has about one cold month, not enough for heavy tweeds."

"I imagine they were woven for the English climate," Mr. Cartwright murmured.

"This cotton goods is nice but more costly than in the Brenham stores," said Pa.

"Yes, I had to pay a high American duty," apologized Mr. Cartwright.

"These guns," said Pa, picking up one, "are cheap; too cheap. A man here needs a good gun. You will find Texans willing to pay a good price for the right kind of gun." Karl began to feel sorry for Mr. Cartwright. He wished Pa would say something pleasant about the things. He was glad when Pa looked at the books.

"I wish my wife could see these. She is the reader in our family. These will sell well." Then he went to the box of queer, folded, ribbon-tied cloth bags. "Himmel! What is this?" He held one dangling from his big hand.

Mr. Cartwright laughed. "Glengarry bonnets, sir, Scottish caps. They are all the fashion for young boys in London now. Here, lad, let me show you!"

He put one of the funny little caps on Karl. The folds opened out so that it fit close to the top of his head. Mr. Cartwright turned him so that he could look at himself in the mirror of the bureau.

Karl looked in horror. The cap was so small it

covered only a part of his head. There was a peak in front and in back and down the back hung short ribbon streamers. There was a bright pin at one side. It was terrible! Karl pulled it off with a sheepish grin. If London boys wore caps like that they sure must be crazy!

Pa looked over all the things again slowly, pricing and examining. "I am not a rich man, Mr. Cartwright, and because of the dry summer the cotton crop is small this year," he said. "I must buy very carefully."

"Of course," said Mr. Cartwright. "I don't expect *anyone* to buy what he does not need."

"I know that," said Pa kindly. "Well, a couple of yards of the blue ribbon for my wife. I always like to take her a little gift. And this book, *Caledonian Songs and Ballads*. She reads aloud to us in the evenings."

"What about a bonnet for the lad? I could let you have it for fifty cents. It is good wool. Queen Victoria loves Scotland. The Royal Princes often wear Glengarry bonnets."

Karl shook his head vigorously at Pa behind Mr. Cartwright's back but Pa didn't see him. In dismay Karl heard Pa say, "Yes, give me one for Karl. He needs a cap for school."

Karl gasped. "Oh, Pa, no! You promised to buy me a big hat! A *big* hat, Pa!"

"Karl!" said Pa in his deep stern voice, the voice that must be obeyed without protest. But Karl *had* to protest!

"I can't wear that cap! It's silly!"

"Silence, young man!" said Pa deep and quiet. "No more." Karl was silent. He knew it was useless to say anything more. He turned his back so that Pa and Mr. Cartwright would not see his tears.

"Don't buy it if the lad doesn't want it, Mr. Zorn," said Mr. Cartwright. "Don't take it to help me."

"Nonsense!" said Pa. "It is a good cap and well worth the money. Thank Mr. Cartwright and tell him good-bye, Karl."

"Good-bye, sir," mumbled Karl. He left out the thanks but no one noticed. Pa paid Mr. Cartwright and stalked out to the wagon. Karl followed him, choking back his sobs.

Silently they climbed into the wagon, silently they drove away. Finally Pa said, still in that deep slow voice, "You were very rude to Mr. Cartwright, Karl. The young man is trying to make a living. You called that fine cap silly."

"It is silly! It is sissy and silly! You promised me a b-b-big h-h-hat for school and then you bought this silly thing!" The tears came and deep wrenching sobs.

"I said we would see about a hat. I decided the cap would do. It is a good cap and much cheaper than a hat. I was glad to buy it from the young man. We will have no more talk."

Karl did not say another word. He knew that Pa

had decided and would be obeyed. Karl was doomed to wear that cap to school, to church and everywhere. And he would hate it every minute. It wasn't even a regular cap, but a *bonnet*, a bonnet with ribbons and a shiny pin. Women wore bonnets, sunbonnets in the fields, close little dress bonnets for church. And babies wore bonnets with ruffles and bows. What would Bill say? At the horrible idea Karl's tears flowed afresh.

After a while Pa said, in his normal voice, "Now, Karl, be a man. You are too big to cry. Now we go to the store and buy the rest of your things, the cloth for your pants and blouses and the fine new school books."

They drew up at the row of stores in the center of town. Pa got out and tied the team to one of the posts that held up the wooden awning in front of the general store. Karl climbed down over the wheels.

He wiped his face on his sleeve. At least Pa wasn't mad any more. He took Pa's hand and they entered the dim, musty-smelling store. It was full to the doors with groceries and dry goods and tools. Then, in the dimness Karl saw, on top of a pile of saddle blankets, a stack of widebrimmed western hats. He turned his eyes away from them quickly. "I did want a brave hat," he said softly.

· FOUR ·

EARLY ON the morning of the first day of school Karl looked at himself in the mirror in Ma's room. He decided that if he could just keep the cap hidden he would look fine. He liked the stiff new jean pants and the blue gingham blouse that Ma had made. He was barefooted, of course, but all the children would be until the cold weather began. His face was shining and pink from cold water and yellow soap and his fair hair was plastered down slick. He would be all right if only he didn't have to put on that Glengarry bonnet.

Well, maybe he could hide it in the canebrake on the way to school, and pick it up on his way home. He went into the sunny kitchen. Pa was already at the breakfast table and Ma was dishing up.

"Ach, what a stylish son we have!" she said. She wiped her hands on her apron and took him by the shoulders. "Turn around. The new clothes fit fine, don't they? Now let me put on your new cap."

She adjusted it on his head and pushed a lock of hair back under it lovingly. Then she stood back with her hands on her hips. She and Pa both looked at him proudly. They didn't see anything strange about a little tow-headed German boy in Texas wearing a Scotch cap.

"It looks just fine," said Pa a little too heartily. "I bet you will be the only boy in school with a new cap from London."

"Yes, sir," said Karl, not heartily at all. "I will be," he thought. He quickly took off the cap and slid into his chair. He took his red-checked napkin from the ring of polished cow-horn.

"I have to go down the road a piece to see about a horse," said Pa. "I'll give you a lift to school."

"Yes, sir," said Karl again. His heart sank. There would be no chance then to hide the cap on the way

to school. Maybe he could hide it in his stack of books. He took as long as he could over breakfast. He asked for extra helpings of pancakes and syrup. He fussed for a long time piling his books on the big geography—his McGuffey's third reader, his slate and slate pencil and one of the new prize pencils.

Pa called several times from the wagon before he dragged himself out and climbed on the seat. They drove out of the lot and down the road much too quickly for Karl's liking. He'd just as soon they drove to school by way of Austin!

When they turned into the main road they saw Bill Riley and his sister, Katy, and Tom Carr, Bill's shadow, walking toward school. They all had on

clean new clothes but Bill was wearing his old big hat. It had achieved just the right creases and dips to look like a ranchman's hat.

Pa slowed up the horses. "Hello, there! Want a lift? Climb in back. It's clean."

Karl's heart sank lower. No use hiding the cap now!

Bill and Katy and Tom climbed in back and stood up, holding onto the back of the seat. " 'Lo, Karl. Good morning, Mr. Zorn," they said.

" 'Lo," said Karl.

"All ready for school?" asked Pa.

"Yes, sir," said Bill respectfully, and then in a different tone, "What you got on, Karl?"

"A cap," said Karl briefly.

"A Glengarry Scotch bonnet, imported from London," said Pa in his deep hearty voice. "There," thought Karl. "It's out! Bonnet!"

"Yes, sir, a Scotch bonnet." Bill's voice was deceptively respectful. "A sure 'nuff bonnet with nice ribbons and pretty pin."

"It's downright purty," said Tom, following Bill's lead. "I bet Katy wishes she had a bonnet like that."

Pa didn't know Bill and Tom the way Karl did. He looked real pleased. "Queen Victoria's sons wear them," he said. Karl managed a wavering smile.

But he was glad when they drove up to the schoolhouse and Pa let them out. Karl kept the little smile rather determinedly as Pa drove off and the teasing became open and noisy.

"Say, come here!" shouted Bill. "Everybody come see the be-yew-tiful lady's bonnet, just like Queen Victoria's! Never saw anything like it, ribbons and pins and all!" The children gathered around and Karl stood stiffly, the smile frozen on his face.

"Lad, turn around and let them see the bally ribbons. My word, by Jove," crowed Bill in what he thought was an English accent. He made a snatch at the ribbons; Karl made a snatch at the cap. His books and slate fell to the ground, pencils rolled away and papers blew over the schoolyard.

"Save the pretty bonnet," gibed Bill and some of the other boys began to chant, "Karl wears a bonnet! Karl wears a bonnet!"

There wasn't any use to try to fight. There were too many against him. Besides Karl didn't *feel* brave as long as he had that cap on. It wasn't worth fighting for. Just then the school bell rang. The boys ran off and Karl began to gather up his things.

"Here is the nice pencil," said a soft voice. It was Ramon Ruiz. Karl took the pencil silently. He folded the cap and put it between his books and followed Ramon into the school.

Once inside, it was better. The first day of school was always fun. Everyone looked different and taller than last spring. Mr. Adams' beard looked longer and fuller. He brushed it down with the same careful gesture.

Mr. Adams had his violin with him and was tuning it as the children came in. "Good," thought Karl. He liked the opening exercises when they sang to the music of the violin. They always started with *Old Hundred* and Karl's voice rose high in "Praise God from whom all blessings flow." Then they sang *America* and finished with *Dixie*.

They got out their new books and settled down to work. For long stretches Karl could forget about that awful cap. At recess he left it folded between his books on the shelf. Bill called, "Don't forget your bonnet, Miss Carlotta," but no one took him up with his teasing. They were organizing a game of *Hot Ball* and Karl was a good catcher. When they divided into sides and each threw the ball as hot and hard as he could, Karl could almost always catch it, no matter how hard it came. He was having so much fun that when he fumbled and Bill yelled, "Catch it in your bonnet," he didn't mind—much.

After school he stopped a minute to ask Mr. Adams about an arithmetic problem, not because he needed to, but to give the rest time to leave the school grounds. The cap was carefully folded in his geography.

On the way home he thought about his problem. He passed the canebrake where he had meant to hide his bonnet but now that everyone had seen it that wouldn't help. He wasn't going to act scared to wear it.

The trouble was that the bonnet was his worst enemy. He couldn't *feel* brave and able to stand up to Bill and the other boys when he was wearing that sissy thing. If he had been wearing a big hat he would have felt as brave as a Texas hero. But of course if he were wearing the hat he wouldn't be pestered. He sighed. He'd just have to try to *pretend* he was wearing the hat and go about his business. He pulled the bonnet out from his books and set it on his head, cocked over one eye, and started whistling *Dixie* as hard as he could. Ma heard him coming and smiled to hear him so cheerful. "School days," thought Ma, "are such a happy time." Karl could have told her differently.

Outwardly Karl's new idea worked. The next morning, when Bill started his teasing, Karl cocked the cap jauntily on one side and just stood with his hands in his pockets and smiled. He looked so pleased with himself that the boys didn't get much fun out of teasing him. But, inside, Karl felt as miserable as ever. He still thought the bonnet was a ridiculous thing. If some other boy had been wearing it he would have been as amused as Bill and his followers, though he would have been kinder about it.

But by his outward indifference he won some relief from teasing. For days there would be nothing said and Karl would have peace. Then Bill would get bored and begin to pester him, and others would follow Bill's lead.

There was the morning when Bill came to school with a baby cap on his head, with the lawn strings hanging down behind. "Look, Karl," he said. "The latest from Paris." The other children snickered. "Don't you want to buy it?"

"I've got a cap," Karl said quietly. "That one looks nice on *you*, Bill." The others laughed at Bill, then, and he left Karl alone.

There was one hard day when Mr. Adams saw the cap for the first time. Karl always took it off before he went inside. This day he was surrounded by jeering boys clear up to the school steps and he wasn't going to please them by taking it off. Mr. Adams called from the window, "Don't be so silly, Karl. What is that funny hat you have on? Give it back to the girl it belongs to and stop acting like a clown."

The boys whooped. Karl said, "I can't. It's mine. I have to wear it." After school he explained to Mr. Adams about the cap, about how hard up Mr. Cartwright was and how Pa had bought it and was proud of it. And how anyway it was the only cap he had.

Mr. Adams said, "I see. You've got quite a problem. Even I never saw a cap like that before. Well, I think you are meeting things in the best way. And, Karl, it takes much more courage to wear the cap than a big hat. It takes bravery to be different."

Karl left Mr. Adams feeling better. It helped to have someone understand. But he didn't feel brave and he didn't want to be different. In the spring he could go back to his old straw hat and maybe next year Pa would get the big hat. Next year seemed a long way off.

· FIVE ·

KARL SAT on the bench of the railroad station and listened to the men all talking at once. Pa had gotten word that the *Mississippi*, the immigrant ship, had reached New Orleans two days ago and would be in Galveston soon. It was Saturday, so he and Karl had driven in to town early to see if the immigrants had arrived.

It had been raining all week but the skies were clearing now and though the drive had been over muddy roads and under dripping trees, it had been through wavering January sunshine.

When they reached Brenham they went first to Mr. Cartwright's office but Mrs. Heine, his landlady, said that Mr. Cartwright had gone to Navasota and couldn't get back on account of swollen streams. "Better go over to the railroad station and see what news has come over the telegraph," she suggested.

So here they were at the station and here were most of the men of Brenham, it seemed—the mayor, the storekeeper and others who were expecting immi-

44

grants. The air was heavy with dampness, dirt and the smell of old cinders.

"Glad to see you, Zorn," said the mayor. "The immigrants have landed at Galveston but heaven knows when they will be here. The bridge over the Brazos between here and Hempstead is washed out and the trains can't go through. And Cartwright is marooned in Navasota. He is trying to get down to meet them."

"Bad, bad!" said Pa. "A bad welcome for the newcomers."

"The down train will come through soon," said the mayor, who seemed to be running things. "It will go as far as the Brazos and meet the train coming up. The passengers will have to be ferried across. It may take some time. Some of us are going down in case Cartwright doesn't get there."

"Yes," said Pa. "They may need us. I'll take the team over to the livery stable and send word by the mail carrier to Mrs. Zorn." He looked at Karl. Karl looked back at him and hoped he wasn't going to leave him in town, too. "I am afraid I will *have* to take you with me," Pa said solemnly, but there was a twinkle in his eye.

"Yes *sir!*" Karl agreed. A train ride as well as seeing the immigrants!

"What about food?" asked the storekeeper. "No telling how long that crossing will take. I'll get crackers and cheese from the store."

45

"There is the milk that can't be sent south," said the mayor. The hotelkeeper offered cups and knives and someone else a basket of apples. There was a sudden hustle and bustle. Pa left Karl at the station and helped to carry over the things from the store and hotel, then put up the team and hurried back just as the train pulled in. He swung Karl up and they all crowded on and the train lumbered off.

Karl looked from the train window at the dreary country outside. Everything was brown or gray. The grass was dead and brown and the moss that hung from the trees was dark and wet looking.

Texas wouldn't look like much to the immigrants, he thought. He wished that they were seeing it first in spring. Then all the leaves would be out and the dogwood and redbud would be in blossom and the fields a gay pattern of wild flowers. January was a dead month. They wouldn't like it much now, he was sure.

It wasn't far to the Brazos. They all got out of the train and walked down toward the ferry. Karl looked at the river. The last time he saw it was in the summer when it was a little trickle in the middle of a wide yellow river bed. Now the bed was filled from bank to bank with the swift brown water hurrying down to the Gulf of Mexico. Karl thought that the short ride across on the ferry was like a sea voyage.

He held Pa's hand and again he wondered how it would look to the newcomers.

They landed in a grove of live oaks where the ground was packed and fairly dry under the dense trees. The men sat on stumps and logs but Karl couldn't sit still. He walked to the track and looked down it toward Hempstead. So he was the first to see the train in the distance.

"Here they come!" he yelled, jumping up and down. The men came forward with the mayor at their head to meet the newcomers.

The first to get off was Mr. Cartwright. He looked tired and worn and not nearly as spick-and-span as usual. "Good of you to come," he said. "I managed to meet the train down the line. This is my cousin, Joseph McBride, who came over with our people."

Mr. McBride was a different kind of Englishman from Mr. Cartwright. He was thin and sharp-featured and dapper, but he looked tired too. Karl only gave him a glance. He was watching the immigrants as they straggled from the train and stood about in groups. There were women with shawls over their heads and children holding to their mothers' skirts. There were big brawny men and little pale city-bred men. They all carried baggage, bags and rolls of bedding, bundles and portmanteaus and boxes. There were boys, too, Karl noticed, some near his own age. They all looked around, up at the moss-laden trees,

down at the brown swollen river. They just stood and waited.

Mr. Cartwright raised his voice. "We will have to wait here to be ferried across the river. Make yourselves as comfortable as you can. These citizens of your new home have come to welcome you."

Most of the immigrants bowed or nodded their heads in greeting. But there was also a murmur and grumbling from some of the men.

"Bad management," one rough voice said. "You bring us so far and land us in a wilderness. Is this your fine Texas?"

Mr. Cartwright said patiently, "We couldn't help the rains, Mr. Owens. Please try to find seats and be patient. These gentlemen have brought us a lunch."

Most of the people sat down quietly. Some sat on their boxes, some spread out bedding and sat on it. But some of the men kept up their loud protests. "It is an imposition! We demand to be taken to our homes *at once!*" Mr. Cartwright tried to quiet them.

Pa and Karl and some of the others started passing out cups of milk to the children, and the store-keeper passed around crackers and cheese. Karl was kept pretty busy because there were over a hundred immigrants and not enough cups and he had to run back and forth with the cups. People said, "Thank you," quietly. It was all so different from what Karl had expected. He had thought all the newcomers would be happy and excited.

Meanwhile the little ferry was taking a few immigrants at a time over the river to the train waiting at the other side. Mr. McBride rounded up the complaining men and took them over first.

"Poor Joseph," said Mr. Cartwright, as he poured out more milk. "He has had them ever since they left England and they have been fussing about everything all the way over. It is partly Joseph's fault. He promised them too much. They expect to be kings in this new land."

"Most of the people are quiet and well-behaved,"

said Pa. "It must be hard, this delay at the end of a long journey."

"I had to cross three ferries to get to them," Mr. Cartwright said impatiently. "I haven't slept for two nights. All they have to do is to sit in this romantic spot in the sunshine."

Pa smiled slowly. "Not romantic for them, I guess,'" he said. "The big trees, that heavy Spanish moss and the cruel-looking river. I remember at first I found it awesome."

After he finished passing milk, Karl wandered around. He would have liked to talk to people and make them feel welcome, but he was too shy. He wondered which men were to come to their farm. Now he began to notice separate immigrants. There were all kinds. There were shabby families and neat ones, rough faces and gentle ones. There was a little old lady, neat as a pin, sitting on a log, knitting as quietly as if she were in her own parlor. One family sat around a blanket, having a regular picnic with their crackers and cheese and apples. Two little girls with shawls over their heads sat close to their mother, watching with big wondering eyes all that went on.

Over near the river a boy about Karl's age was throwing sticks into the water below. His bright red hair showed from the edge of his cap and his quick blue eyes were watching the loading of the ferry.

, Karl sat down by him and threw sticks in the river too.

"Yon's a mighty river," said the boy. "Looks almost as mighty as the Thames."

"He doesn't talk like Mr. Cartwright," thought Karl and asked, "Are you English?"

"Scottish," said the boy.

"Oh," said Karl. Then he explained, "That's the Brazos River. It is bigger now because of the floods. Sometimes it is almost dry."

"Any Red Indians aboot here?" asked the boy eagerly.

"No-o," said Karl. He didn't add that he had never seen an Indian. "But there are alligators further down."

"Alligators! Mon! Mon!" The blue eyes were open wide.

"Alligators and rattlesnakes and water moccasins. And there are coyotes and wolves in the woods." Karl was trying to make Texas sound as attractive as possible.

"D'ye ride wild horses?" asked the boy with interest.

"Yes, I ride," said Karl modestly, though old Bessie was not in the least wild. "And rope cattle." Well, he told himself, he *had* roped a calf.

"I hope there will be cattle on the ranch where we

are to go," said the boy. Then he chuckled. "Fancy my dad roping cattle!"

"Where do you go?" asked Karl. He hoped it would be somewhere near him. He liked this eager boy with his funny way of talking.

"To a mon named Zorn," answered the boy.

"Is your name Gordon and do you have a big brother?" asked Karl in excitement.

"I'm Jock Gordon," said the boy. "But there is no brither. Just my dad and mither. Why?"

"I'm Karl Zorn. You are coming to our place!" The two boys grinned at each other.

"On your ranch!" Jock breathed. "Will you teach me to ride and rope and hunt?"

"Yes, indeed," said Karl. Later he would have to explain the difference between a farm and a ranch, but not yet! He felt very big and brave and Western. "We'll have fun! Pa thought you would be grown up," he said. "He wanted two men to help him, but, Himmel! I am glad you are not!" Then he asked, "Which are your folks?"

"Yon they sit." Jock pointed to a couple sitting a little apart from the others. The woman was sturdy looking with a round rosy face and curly red hair, only a little darker than Jock's. The wiry little man sitting beside her had Jock's eager face and quick manner. He looked as if he had just perched on that log for a minute and would be off on something interesting as soon as he got his breath.

"He doesn't look like a farmer," said Karl.

"Eh, but he is," Jock said quickly. "We had a wee bit of a farm in Scotland afore we lost it and came to London. Come on and meet them."

"This is Karl Zorn," said Jock to his parents.

"Sae this is the laird's son," said Mr. Gordon with a twinkle. Karl grinned. First he was a rancher and now a laird's son, whatever that was! Mrs. Gordon just took his hand and smiled at him. Then, as someone called from the ferry, she picked up one of the bundles and started forward with a quick free step. Karl and Jock and Mr. Gordon took the rest of the baggage and followed her.

Pa was at the ferry, helping people get into the boat. Karl jerked at his coat.

"Pa, this is Mr. and Mrs. Gordon—and Jock."

Pa nodded to them. "Glad to see you," he said. He looked beyond them as if for the older son he had expected.

Karl added, "Pa, you didn't get two workers, but, listen, Pa, I got me a boy!"

· SIX ·

ON THE TRAIN back to Brenham the two boys sat together and chattered happily. It was Karl who talked the most, telling Jock all about Texas. He told about the farm and the cattle and the horses. He didn't say that the principal crop was cotton—that didn't sound exciting. He told about the prairies in the spring but he didn't say anything about the summer heat. He told all about camp meeting but he left out the fact that he got tired of it. If he stretched things it was because Jock had started out with a bad view of Texas and Karl wanted him to love it.

Everyone was talking in the coach. The Texans who had ordered immigrants were seeking them out and talking to them. And the immigrants themselves seemed more cheerful and talkative now they were near their destination.

Mr. Cartwright came by, looking worried. He stopped where Pa sat with the Gordons. Pa explained about Jock being a little boy and not the worker they had expected. "I think I can find you another man later," said Mr. Cartwright. "There have had to be

some shiftings and changes. Too many," he sighed.

"Still having trouble with those fellows?" Pa asked.

"Having trouble with others, too," admitted Mr. Cartwright. "Joseph promised them all sorts of things that simply aren't so. He told one family that they would be near the town and they refuse to go to the place assigned because it is five miles out."

Pa's chuckle rumbled. "That is a matter of geography. Five miles isn't far in Texas. I suppose it is a long way in England."

"Some expect homes without having to work for them. I think it is mostly the fault of the malcontents. They have stirred up some of the good people." Mr.

Cartwright hesitated. "We may have more trouble after we get in. Some of the planters are disgusted. There may have to be reassignments. Mr. Zorn, could you stay in town tonight in case we need help? Mrs. Schmidt has told me anyone who had to stay in town could stay at her boardinghouse. You and the Gordons could stay there."

Pa thought a minute. "If someone is going up our way and can take word to my wife so she won't worry. Sure, son, I'll be glad to help." Karl was glad. It would be awful to leave in the midst of the excitement.

When they got to Brenham, Pa took Karl and the Gordons to Mrs. Schmidt's boardinghouse right downtown. It was crude but clean. The walls were plain unfinished lumber, the floors were bare and the furniture was scanty. But the beds were clean and, Mr. Cartwright said, the food was good. "I stayed here myself when I first came to Brenham," he said as he helped Mrs. Gordon up the steps.

Karl was glad to be there. He was pretty tired and he was glad they wouldn't have the long drive home tonight. Mrs. Gordon looked glad, too, as she took off her shawl and bonnet. Karl liked her wavy red hair and her quiet blue eyes. They all had supper in the big dining room—ham and grits and sorghum molasses. Then the men went over to Mr. Cartwright's office to see if they were needed.

After supper Karl and Mrs. Gordon and Jock sat with the other boarders on the front gallery and talked. Mrs. Gordon, in her soft burring voice, told Karl about her girlhood in Scotland—the little cottage on the moors with the sheep grazing and "the kye coming home in the gloaming." Karl thought that in spite of the queer words country life in Scotland was not so different from country life as he knew it.

Others of the immigrants who would be sent to their destinations tomorrow were brought in and, after they had eaten, joined the little group on the gallery. The little old lady with her knitting was there, and the two scared-looking little girls with their mother. They sat on the steps together with their frightened eyes on the strange tree-shaded street. It all seemed very peaceful.

By-and-by someone started singing and they all joined in. Karl was surprised that they knew the same songs he did—*Ben Bolt* and *Annie Laurie* and *Coming through the Rye*.

The pleasantness was interrupted as Mr. Cartwright and Pa brought a new group up the walk. This was a large dirty family led by Mr. Owens, who had made trouble at the ferry. He took one look at the clean, bare hall and roared at Mr. Cartwright.

"We will not stay in this pigsty! You promised to get us to our destination. If you can't do that take us to a reputable place!"

"This place is quite respectable. If you had gone to the man who was waiting for you, Mr. Owens, you would be home by now." Mr. Cartwright's voice was very patient.

"The man expected my wife to work for him and take care of his children. Who would take care of our children, I'd like to know! I demand to be taken to a better place with decent people!"

"I'll take you to the hotel," said Mr. Cartwright quietly. He stopped and spoke to Mrs. Schmidt, standing indignant in the doorway. "Thank you and forgive us for disturbing you." He left with his noisy troupe following him.

The little old lady with the knitting gave a contemptuous sniff. "Pigsty, he says! I've seen the cellar where they lived in London. That young man is too good to them. They think they are important now."

Pa lingered a minute. "They will shake down into place, but it is hard for Mr. Cartwright. He is afraid the venture will get a bad name and he won't be able to live this down. Some of the men are going up and down the street abusing Mr. Cartwright and his cousin and trying to hire out to anyone they see." He shook his head, then added more cheerfully, "I've found a young man for our farm."

"What I dinna like," said Mrs. Gordon in her gentle voice, "is that they gie us all a bad name. Brenham will long mind the night the immigrants came and forget that most of us were quiet and biddable." She sighed. "I will be gey glad when we get out in the country where it is peaceful."

The old lady chuckled. "We expected Texas to be rough and wild, but it is our own people who are that."

The earlier peace was gone. They all sat and listened to the noises of the town. Once there was loud shouting near the square and once a man came to the gate and yelled, "They will take you to the

hotel if you demand it! You don't have to stay here!"
and then dashed off into the darkness.

Finally everything quieted down. Pa and Mr.
Gordon came back. With them was a big sullen-
looking young man. Pa introduced him to Mrs.
Schmidt. "This is Jim Dark. It is late, I know, but can
you give this young man something to eat? He is
going out to the farm with me in the morning."

Mrs. Schmidt took the man to the dining room.
Mrs. Gordon turned a troubled face toward Pa. "But
wasna he one of the troublemakers, Mr. Zorn?"

"Yes," Pa said. "It seemed best to separate him
from the other men in town. The man he was to go
to refused to take him after all the trouble. He is
young and was influenced by the other men. He will
not be a nuisance to your family. We will give him a
room in the house with us."

"You are a good mon, Mr. Zorn," said Mrs. Gordon. Karl thought so too. "I hope he does not make
any more trouble."

"He will be fine," said Pa. "The poor young man
expected a land of milk and honey, and all he found
was Texas mud. Some day he will know that the soil
of his new land can provide the milk and honey." He
stifled a yawn. "Everything is quiet now, though
poor Mr. Cartwright had to pay for a lot of the
rogues to stay at the hotel. As soon as Jim eats we

can all go to bed and get an early start in the morning. We ought to be home by nine."

"Hame! That sounds pleasant." Mrs. Gordon rose. "Come, laddie, tae bed. And in the morn we will be *hame!*"

· SEVEN ·

WHEN KARL came down to breakfast Monday morning he heard Ma and Mrs. Gordon talking fit to kill as they fixed breakfast. Yesterday the newcomers had spent most of the time down at the little cabin, getting settled and resting from their long trip. Jim Dark was given a room in the house and stayed there most of the day. They all came together for meals but yesterday Ma had treated them like company. Today Mrs. Gordon had on a calico dress and a big apron and the men were in work clothes and came in from the barn with Pa.

Ma and Mrs. Gordon seemed to hit it off fine. Karl thought he hadn't seen Ma looking so bright and happy since the camp meeting. She must have been as lonesome for woman-talk as he had been for a boy to play with. Jock was all ready for school with his red hair dark with water and his cap and slate waiting on a chair.

"Now this is fine, fine!" said Pa heartily from his end of the table as Ma sat down behind the coffee-pot at the other end. "We've got a nice big family,

63

haven't we, Ma?" Mr. and Mrs. Gordon sat at one side of the table and Jim and the boys sat at the other.

Ma smiled. "Give your big family some sausage and eggs, Rudolph, and let us eat. The boys have to get to school and Mrs. Gordon and I have many, many things to do." She didn't sound flustered and worried but as if she were looking forward to the work ahead.

After breakfast Karl picked up his books and the Glengarry cap. He hated to put it on. He waited until he and Jock were outside. What would Jock think? Karl had worn his old straw hat on the trip to get the immigrants because the weather had been bad. After all his bragging to Jock it was a comedown to put on that silly cap. It didn't fit the picture he had drawn of himself as a riding, roping Westerner.

Jock noticed the cap at once. "You have a Glengarry bonnet," he said.

"Uh-huh," Karl grunted. "Pa bought it from Mr. Cartwright and I have to wear it." He waited for the teasing comment that he was sure Jock would make.

" 'Tis a fine braw one," said Jock, and to his amazement Karl heard the same admiration in his voice as when Karl had told him about his riding. "I have been wanting one but Dad couldna buy it."

"That's right," Karl thought, "both Jock and the bonnet are Scotch."

"I wanted a big hat, like all the big brave men wear —cowboys and sheriffs and heroes," said Karl.

"And is the bonnet no a braw cap?" asked Jock. "Most of the Highland regiments wear them."

"Soldiers?" asked Karl. "Do soldiers wear bonnets with streamers on them?"

"Of course," said Jock. " 'Tis a bonnie sight to see a company of Highlanders come marching doon the street with the pipes playing and their kilts and sporrans swinging and their ribbons blowing. 'Tis a sight to warm the heart. And, lad, there are no braver fighters!"

He began to sing and marched in time to his singing:

"Our sodger lads look'd braw, look'd braw
Wi' their tartans, kilts, an' a', an' a',
Wi' their bonnets, an' feathers, an' glitterin' gear,
An' pibroch soundin' sweet and clear."

Karl marched along with him. The gay lilting tune and the idea that soldiers wore bonnets were lifegiving, like the fresh morning breeze that was blowing in their faces. But he stopped Jock's singing to ask questions. What was a kilt? And a sporran? And a pibroch? And were the bonnets *just* like his own?

By the time they drew near school Karl knew all

about kilts. Skirts! Short pleated plaid skirts worn by soldiers! And about sporrans, great fur purses that hung from the belt. And about the bagpipes that played pibrochs, wild martial music. It was all so exciting, Karl hardly noticed Bill and Tom sitting on the school fence.

"Him and his silly bonnet!" scoffed Bill. Karl heard him but he paid no attention. Now he did not have the ashamed sinking feeling about his cap. Bill was just ignorant. He didn't know that soldiers wore caps like this one. And Jock liked it! Karl cocked his cap at a jaunty angle and led Jock across the yard to Mr. Adams, standing at the school door.

"Oh, this is one of the newcomers," said Mr. Adams. "We have several others." Karl saw a big girl he had noticed with the immigrants and the two little frightened girls, sitting together under a tree, still frightened, still big-eyed and silent. Others had gone to schools on the other side of town. "Welcome, Jock," added Mr. Adams, and began to ring his handbell for school to start.

At supper that night Karl said eagerly, "Pa, did you know that soldiers in Scotland wear Glengarry bonnets?"

"So?" said Pa. "Well, that is natural. They are Scotch cap." He helped himself to a biscuit and passed the plate to Mr. Gordon.

"Not only sodgers," said Mr. Gordon in his quick

voice. "Mony men do. And the gentry, when they dress for great occasions, wear them with their kilts."

"Think of that, Karl!" said Ma. "Grown men in their best!" She smiled at him. Why, Ma had known how he hated the cap! thought Karl.

"I thought they were only for little boys," he said.

"The Scottish bonnet is not a child's cap," Mrs. Gordon spoke up. "Think of the heroes who have worn them, fighters and rebels and clansmen. Rob Roy, perhaps, and Bruce and Douglas and the Bonnie Prince himself, hiding in the heather."

"Did they all wear Glengarries with fancy pins and ribbons on them?" Karl wanted to ask about these heroes, who they were and what they did and why the prince was hiding, but first he had to get things clear about the cap.

"Either that or the Balmoral, like a flat cap, or the Kilmarnock, like a baggy tam-o-shanter," said Mr. Gordon. "But they all wore brooches and ribbons or pom-pons. And each clansman wore a sprig of a plant stuck in his cap—his family crest; heather or pine or a bit of gorse."

"Flowers, too, with pins and ribbons," breathed Karl. He thought if he had had to wear a bit of willow or mesquite in his cap he would have died. "And they were fighting men!"

"The verra bravest," said Mr. Gordon. He didn't know why Karl was so interested but he liked talking about his homeland. "Eh, lad, d'ye no ken the Scottish ballads of their doings?"

By that time supper was finished. Ma said, "Ballads!" She went to the little bookcase in the front room and came back with the book Pa had bought on that fateful day when he had bought the bonnet. "*Caledonian Poems and Ballads*. Were these what you meant?" She handed the book to Mr. Gordon.

"Aye. Caledonia is the old name for Scotland." Mr. Gordon turned the pages eagerly, looking for his favorites. Jim Dark pushed back his chair and went outside. He had not seemed interested in their talk. He didn't seem interested in anything, Karl thought.

"Let's hear some of them," said Pa. "I believe in following things up when you are interested. Will you read some of them, Gordon?"

"Mither reads best," said Mr. Gordon.

"Na, na. I maun help Mrs. Zorn with the dishes," said his wife. "We can listen as we work."

Ma and Mrs. Gordon cleared the table. Then they put on the cloth that covered the table between meals and Ma lighted the lamp and set it in the center. They worked quietly as Mr. Gordon put on his spectacles and began to read.

In the quiet room Mr. Gordon read on and on, one after another of the old ballads he loved so well. His Scottish voice gave out all the rich beauty of the words. Karl sat with pulses beating to the exciting battles, his ears ringing to the sound of trumpets, the clash of claymores.

All the rest of his life Karl remembered that evening. It was a turning point when new excitement and beauty entered his life. He knew the heroes of his own land. Now he discovered a new land and a new gallery of heroes.

Mr. Gordon read,

> *"Scots, wha hae wi' Wallace bled,*
> *Scots, wham Bruce has aften led,"*

and then stopped to tell of the brave deeds of those two heroes. "Bruce was a leader even after his death," he said. " 'Tis told that he ordered the brave Douglas to take his heart to the Holy Land, and in battle Douglas flung the heart before him." He turned the pages rapidly. "Here it is—

> *'Then in his stirrups up he stood*
> *So lion-like and bold,*
> *And held the precious Heart aloft*
> *All in its case of gold.*
>
> *He flung it from him, far ahead*
> *And never spake he more,*
> *But— "Pass thee first, thou gallant Heart*
> *As thou wert wont of yore!"' "*

But best of all Karl liked the two poems with the bonnets in them. There was the bonnet of Bonnie Dundee—

"Come fill up my cup, come fill up my can,
Come saddle your horses and call up your men;
Come open your gates and let me gae free,
For it's up wi' the bonnets of Bonnie Dundee!"

The other poem was even more exciting. Mr. Gordon did not read it as a poem but sang it to its stirring

music. Jock and Mrs. Gordon joined in and even
Karl followed the lilt of it—

> *"Trumpets are sounding,*
> *War-steeds are bounding,*
> *Stand to your arms and march in good order;*
> *England shall many a day*
> *Tell of the bloody fray,*
> *When the blue-bonnets came over the Border!"*

Karl could see the kilts and ribbons, he could hear
the pipes! What a game it would make! Karl could
hardly wait for tomorrow to come to start it.

There was another game in the story of Prince Charles Stuart who claimed the British throne. He came to Scotland and the clans followed him until they were defeated in the great battle of Culloden. But through all his troubles they remained faithful to him and hid him in the heather and in caves, though there was a great reward offered for him. Mr. Gordon sang *Charlie, He's My Darling*, the song that the people sang about the prince. They always loved him and called him "Bonny Prince Charlie" and "The Young Chevalier." Karl knew just the place where Charlie could hide in the heather.

The dishes were long ago finished and Ma and Mrs. Gordon had joined them around the table. Ma had her sewing but Mrs. Gordon just listened, her eyes as bright as the boys'. Karl's brain whirled with the music and the heroic words and the throng of new heroes in the plain old Texas kitchen.

Finally Pa said, "That's enough for tonight. We can't read the book at one time. There is work to do tomorrow, and school. Thank you, Gordon."

Karl rubbed his eyes. He came back from Scotland and remembered arithmetic problems he should have done. He would have to get up early tomorrow and do them. The Gordons went out to their cabin and Jim came in and went to his room. Karl went upstairs and undressed in the dark. His mind was a muddle of claymores and tartans, of wild Highlanders and of lowland border raiders. As he snuggled down under the patchwork quilt he was murmuring the words of the song that seemed right at home in Texas—"All the blue bonnets are over the border."

· EIGHT ·

KARL AND JOCK could hardly wait the next morning to get through breakfast and start to school so that they could be alone together. Their minds were full of the tales and songs of the night before and each had vast plans to tell the other. They began talking at the same time as they turned out of the farmyard into the road.

"We can be Douglas," Jock said. "Fighting the enemy and casting the heart of Bruce before him!"

"And Bonnie Prince Charlie hiding in the heather," added Karl. "And have raids across the border!" The days stretched before them, full of exciting possibilities.

"And, what about having a clan ourselves?" asked Jock. "With secret signs. And a badge to wear in our bonnets." Then he added, "But I have no bonnet, no braw Scottish cap."

"You could buy one from Mr. Cartwright," said Karl eagerly. It would be nice if Jock had a cap like his. "He had a lot in a box—about a dozen."

"No money," said Jock briefly. Of course, Karl

thought, if the Gordons had money to buy fancy caps they would not have come so far from home to be farm workers. The Zorns didn't have much money but Jock's family didn't have *any*. He said, "That is so. I tell you, next time we go to town, we'll go see Mr. Cartwright. Maybe you could earn a cap someway."

"I could! I could! Maybe sweep his office or take care of his horse or run errands for him! I'd do anything to get a bonnet. Then we could be a clan, just we two."

"It would be fun to have a big clan," said Karl. "For battles and forays. Maybe some of the other boys would join."

"No," said Jock firmly. "They are not worthy. Making fun of your bonnie cap!" He swung along in a determined manner as if the matter were settled.

"All of them didn't tease," argued Karl. "Just Bill and Tom. We wouldn't want *them*. But more fellows would make everything better."

"No," said Jock firmly. "They laughed, didn't they? They could have stopped Bill. Serve them right to be left out!"

"But—" began Karl. Then he stopped. He knew how it felt to be left out of things. He would like to be one of a big merry gang. But Jock was his friend and he appreciated his championing of his cause.

"Well," he said. "Let's sneak through the heather now."

So the two boys left the road for the tall weeds, and bending low, made their way to school, crouching down when a wagon passed, dashing through open spaces and coming up on the schoolyard panting. "We outwitted the red-coats that time!" Karl thought how much fun it was to have someone to share his games. Some day he would tell Jock about Dr. Brenham and they could play that game too.

Saturday the two boys rode to town with Mr. Zorn. They asked to be put down at Mr. Cartwright's house. Mr. Cartwright was at his desk, checking accounts, but he looked up with his quick smile and offered them both chairs as if they were grown men of business.

"How are things going at the Zorn farm?" he asked. "Is everything satisfactory?" The boys nodded. "Good, I am glad to hear of a place where there are no problems to be settled. Or are there? Did you come to consult me about something wrong?"

"No sir," said Karl. "But Jock wants a Glengarry bonnet like mine."

"I am glad to hear it," said Mr. Cartwright. "I have that big box of them that I have been unable to sell. I'll be glad to have you buy one."

Jock squirmed in his chair. "I canna really buy one, sir. But if you could let me work for one, I'd do anything you need. We want to have a clan and I need a cap to be a clansman."

"I can see that," said Mr. Cartwright gravely. "You must have a cap. Will it be a large clan?" He seemed to have an idea.

"No sir, just the two of us," said Karl.

"We dinna want the ithers," added Jock. He started to add that they had made life hard for Karl about his cap, but Karl kicked his leg suddenly. He didn't want Mr. Cartwright to know how much trouble the cap had cost him.

"I don't have any work you could do," said Mr. Cartwright. "Mrs. Heine keeps my rooms clean and I keep my horse at the livery stable. What I need is a salesman. There are eleven more caps in the box. If you could sell ten I'd be glad to give you the other as your commission."

"How could he sell ten caps?" thought Karl. Remembering how he had objected to his own he didn't see much chance of a large market for them.

But Jock was sitting straight and eager in his chair. "I can do it, sir," he said firmly. "The clan will have twelve members. And they will each have to buy a cap to belong! Can you make me a lower price, since I'm going to sell so many?" Karl looked amazed at Jock's about-face and Mr. Cartwright leaned back in his chair and laughed.

"An American salesman already," he said. "Or is it the Scottish? Yes, I'll lower the price and be glad to, to get rid of those caps." He went to the bedroom and came out with a dark green Glengarry bonnet. "Perhaps if I let you wear yours it would help sales. But if you don't sell all the caps you must pay me for yours."

"Oh, I'll sell them," said Jock confidently. He put the cap on proudly. It looked right on his red hair as Karl's cap had never looked on his tow-colored locks. "You wear it like a Scotsman," said Mr. Cartwright.

They got up to leave. "I'll report to you soon," Jock said. "And thank you, sir."

"Thank *you*," said Mr. Cartwright. "And if you are thinking of starting a gun club or a reading club, please make the purchase of guns and books from me requisite to membership."

The boys laughed. Mr. Cartwright surely did use big words! They ran happily down the street to meet Pa and the team at the store.

The two boys entered into the organization of the clan with equal enthusiasm but with different motives. To Karl the game was the thing and the more boys in it the better it would be. Jock liked the make-believe but his main idea now was selling the caps. They both agreed that they would have to go slowly in recruiting the clan.

Monday morning they appeared at school in their Glengarry bonnets. On their gingham shirts each of them wore a little plaid badge that Ma had made. The letters C.T. on it stood for Clan Texas. Bill noticed all this at once.

"Well, well," he said. "*Two* little bonnet boys. What is the fancy badge about?"

"We cannot tell you," said Karl. "It is very secret."

"You'd not be interested," said Jock. They went past him and sat down on a bench at the side of the yard. Bill looked at them a minute and then walked away. "Silly stuff!" he scoffed.

Some of the other boys gathered around the two clansmen and asked questions. "What is it, a club?" "What is it for?" "Can anyone else belong?"

Before Karl could answer "yes" to the last question Jock spoke. " 'Tis a verra special club. Verra important. What do you think, Karl? Can we admit any more members?"

Karl followed his lead. "Well, maybe. There would have to be a meeting to decide." Then the schoolbell rang and the subject was closed for a time.

At recess, though, it began again. Pee Wee Peters and Ramon Ruiz came up to the two. "Aw, let us join your club," begged Pee Wee in his high voice. Karl remembered Pee Wee had taken no part in the teasing and that Ramon had been the one who had helped him pick up his papers on the terrible first day he had worn the bonnet.

"Shall we?" asked Karl of Jock, as if they had not planned all along to enlarge the Clan. "Aye," agreed Jock. "We might."

Karl nodded. He leaned forward and whispered, "Meet us at the chalk bank at four o'clock."

"Sure," whispered Pee Wee. "The chalk bank. We'll be there."

"Where is this bank?" asked Jock. "In Brenham? We canna go to town."

"You'll see." Karl chuckled. "It's not in town. It's a good secret place for the Clan."

Other boys came up after they heard that Pee Wee and Ramon had been admitted. Karl told them the secret meeting place. He counted them on his fingers. There were eight boys besides himself and Jock. Bill and Tom stood at the other side of the yard, looking contemptuously at the group around Karl. "Baby stuff," scoffed Bill again.

The chalk bank was a perfect meeting place for a secret club. It was exactly what its name implied, a small cave in a bank formed by an outcropping of natural chalk. At the beginning of each school term, or whenever the supply of chalk ran low, some of the fathers would go up to the bank with the boys and pry loose big pieces of chalk. When it was fresh it was damp enough to be molded like clay into long pencil-like sticks or, if dry, it could be whittled into shape. The cave had been made from these repeated quarryings. It wasn't big but the boys could stand in it. The walls were whitish gray with one patch of startling white where the last chalk had been mined. There were bushes around the entrance. Any fugitive chieftain would have been glad of such a refuge.

Jock looked at it with approval. " 'Tis a fine hidey-hole. A good trysting place for the Clan." He poked into the crevices and looked out the doorway. "Here they come," he said.

The boys came up the little path and through the bushes. The cave was a close fit for ten boys, but they sat close, hugging their knees. As soon as they were all there Karl began to tell them about the clans of Scotland and of their bravery and adventures. He repeated as well as he could remember some of the tales he had heard, with Jock prompting him and adding his bit. Karl's enthusiasm and excitement were in his voice and it spread to the other boys. "So we thought we would form a clan in Texas," he ended.

Jock added, "We swear to stick togither and protect the weak. And not to pester ithers," he added sternly. Then he said, "Each clansman maun have a braw Glengarry bonnet. Mr. Cartwright is going to hold all of his and sell them just to us. They will be .35 cents each."

"You mean we can all buy real Scotch caps?"

"Aye, just like Karl's and mine." He took off his bonnet and passed it around. The boys all started talking at once, chattering about ways and means. "I still got some of my birthday money," said Pee Wee. "I can get one right away." "I know how I can earn some," said another. "Me too." "Maybe Mama will give me some," said another hopefully. Money was not plentiful among these farm boys but each was eager to find some way to get together the seven nickles needed.

"Perhaps Mr. Cartwright will let you pay it bit by bit if you have not all the money at once," suggested Jock. He was elated that they all were planning to buy. Karl looked on, gravely smiling. He was thinking of the day Pa had bought the Scotch bonnet for him and how he had hated it; and how these same boys had thought Bill's scoffing at it funny. Now they all wanted one. It was the same cap. It was just a matter of how you looked at it.

He took out his slate and picked up a sliver of chalk from the floor of the cave and began to write the boys' names.

JOCK GORDON	TERRY MURPHY
PEE WEE PETERS	KURT WASSER
RAMON RUIZ	DAVE ABRAMS
NIKLAS PIAST	BEAUREGARD KING
JOE MRAZ	KARL ZORN

Jock looked over his shoulder. "A fine Scottish clan!" He grinned.

"No, a Texas clan," corrected Karl gently. "From many countries, but now all Texans."

Pee Wee squeaked, "Mr. Adams said that 'Texas' means 'Friends' in the Indian language."

"But we have no Indians?" asked Jock solemnly. The boys laughed at the joke.

"The Clan of Friends, that is nice," said Karl. He felt very happy in the midst of this laughing group—all friends now.

Suddenly Jock whispered, "Hark! A skulker in the heather! I hear someone outside the cave."

"It's just me," said a familiar voice. Tom Carr's head appeared at the door of the cave.

Karl stood up. "Let us alone, Tom!" he shouted, all his friendly feelings gone. "Go away!"

"Is Bill with you?" asked Jock belligerently.

"No, just me. Can I come in?" Tom tried to sound as gruff as Bill but he did not.

"Watch him, men!" cautioned Karl. "Come just inside," he added. "Now what do you want?"

"Bill says clubs are silly, but it doesn't sound that way to me." Tom stood inside the entrance and leaned against the wall. He was trying to look careless and indifferent but without Bill's backing he sounded mild, almost friendly.

"You have been listening?" Pee Wee piped.

"Yes, some. It sounded fun. I got four bits at home. Could I buy a cap and put my name on the slate?"

"You, a friend!" scoffed Jock. "You didna act like a friend to Karl!"

"I didn't do nothing. I *could* be real friendly." Karl was amazed. Tom was almost pleading!

"Would you promise?" Karl asked sternly. "And not pester the little boys and not back up Bill?"

"Uh-huh. Bill will be mad at me because I come. If you don't let me in I'll be in a mess all around." Karl felt sorry for him, sorry for Tom Carr!

"Go outside and wait," he said. "The Clan will have to decide."

As soon as Tom had gone everybody talked at

once. Some of the boys remembered his past pestering and wanted to keep Tom out.

"Don't be a softy," grumbled Jock.

"One more cap sold," Karl whispered back.

"Aye, but would he be a traitor to the Clan?" said Jock.

"No," Karl answered. "If Bill is mad at him, he won't be around *him*. Tom will be all right by himself, I do believe, Jock."

After a little more discussion the Clan voted to admit Tom. They called him in. Karl added his name to the list on the slate. Then Tom grinned and the rest grinned back at him.

"Now what do we do?" asked Pee Wee.

"We maun have a chief," said Jock. "I think it should be Karl. He planned the Clan."

"We planned it together," said Karl, but everyone yelled, "Karl! Karl!" so he was elected by acclamation.

Karl was pleased but embarrassed. What did they expect of him now? At the German League Pa had made a speech when he was elected as treasurer. Karl said hesitantly, "Thank you. I will try to be a good chief of Clan Texas. I will lead you in battles, in forays and adventures!" Then he glanced toward the entrance. "Look how low the sun is! I have to get home and help milk!" And all the warriors of Clan Texas hurried home to their evening's chores.

· NINE ·

Jock was faced with a hard problem that looked as if it had no answer. In order to get his own cap free he had to sell ten caps. Counting Tom, he had sold to nine boys. And there weren't any others to sell to; no one else that would fit into the Clan. There were some girls and little boys—and Bill. And the Clan did not want Bill, he was no friend to any of them. Unless some family with a boy of the right age moved into the district there didn't seem to be any way for Jock to sell that last cap.

"We might let girls in," suggested Karl reluctantly. He didn't want to but Jock just *had* to earn that cap! "We'd only have to let one in."

"Just one lass would spoil the Clan," declared Jock. "Women stay at home. They dinna fight."

"There was Flora MacDonald who saved Prince Charlie," suggested Karl. "And Kate Barlass, who bolted the door, and The Lady of the Lake." Mr. Gordon was reading Scott's poem aloud to them in the evenings now.

"Nae lassies," said Jock firmly. "Sometimes we

might let them play with us, but no as members of Clan Texas." Well, it was Jock's problem, Karl thought.

One by one the boys got the money together and bought their caps and wore them to school. As the first ones appeared Bill hooted, "Another sissy baby!" but as more and more of the caps were proudly worn by the boys his hoots died away. He tried to act as if he didn't see them. They were all below his notice! But Karl saw that he was often watching them as members of the Clan gathered on the school grounds. Of course they did not play any of the Clan games at school, but there always seemed to be plans and meeting places to arrange. Karl was in the midst of them. Sometimes he would see Bill standing to one side, looking scornful but also, Karl noticed, slightly puzzled.

Now the cold wet weather of the Texas winter was giving way and spring was blowing in on the south wind. As the weather grew warmer the household at the Zorn farm seemed more and more like one family. Ma and Mrs. Gordon were making themselves percale housedresses. The three men worked together and wore the same kind of blue cotton work shirts, open at the neck and with the sleeves rolled up.

Getting out of his stiff, heavy, foreign-looking clothes seemed to make Jim more human and like one of them. He still didn't have much to say but he no longer looked sullen. Sometimes when he thought he was alone, and particularly when he was with the animals, he whistled softly. The animals seemed to like him and he was especially good with the horses.

One evening Karl was in the back lot and saw Jim driving in the horses from the pasture. He was riding one bareback, trotting easily. As he passed Karl he lifted his hand high and called, "Hey!" Karl waved and said, "Hey!" and waited a minute to see if Jim would say anything else, but he drove the horses on toward the barn. Karl turned toward the house. "Why, Jim almost smiled!" he thought. When Jim came into the house he was the same silent Jim. But

Karl remembered the carefree rider and never felt as strange with Jim after that.

Jock watched the advance of spring across the prairies with amazement—this riot of color that filled the fields and woods and even the ditches by the roadside. First the dogwood and redbud in the woods and then, like a spreading flood, Indian Paintbrush, wine-cups, yellow daisies. Finally came the azure glory of the bluebonnets, spreading up the hills, in pastures, by roadsides and as far as the eye could see, rolling waves of blue.

"Of course, 'tis no as bonnie as the heather," said Jock stoutly to Karl one afternoon, as they walked home from the chalk bank and looked across the hills;

more blue than ever in the twilight. "But this—! 'Tis like all the paint in the world just spilled out across the hills—red and yellow and pink and blue, blue."

He began to whistle *All the Bluebonnets Are Over the Border*. Then an idea stopped him. "I ken what plant will be our Clan badge, what bit of sprig we will wear in our bonnets—the bluebonnet, of course."

"Of course," agreed Karl. "That is just right for a Texas Clan," and he joined in the song. They marched along swinging their jackets over their arms. Each morning it was cool enough for their mothers to bundle them into their jackets, but by the time school was out the sun was beating down and they couldn't bear to wear them. The evenings were longer now and the games could continue later— until home chores called them.

As spring advanced there was a plan growing among the German families around Brenham. The older folks remembered the May Day celebrations in the old country, with songs and dancing and feasting. They decided to have some such celebration here in the new country—an all-day picnic with the town band to play, with all the old-time music and dancing. The children had never seen the old-country celebrations. They listened eagerly to the plans that were discussed wherever people gathered.

"What kind of dancing and singing?" asked Karl one night as they were all sitting on the wide gal-

lery after supper—Pa and Mr. Gordon and Jim
Dark tipped back in their chairs with their feet on
the banisters, Ma and Mrs. Gordon rocking vigorously and the two boys sitting on the steps.

Pa considered a moment. "Oh, I suppose the regular dances, the polka and the schottische. And I hear
some of the young people are planning special dances
in old-country costumes. Singing club groups will
lead the singing."

"Could we dance?" asked Jock eagerly.

"Everyone will dance," said Pa. "Fathers and
mothers and grandfathers and grandmothers, and
down to the littlest kinder."

"No, I mean a special dance," persisted Jock, "of
our ain."

"Like what?" Pa pulled on his pipe and looked at
Jock. He was getting used to Jock's enthusiasms.

"I dinna ken," said Jock. "Just something for us
boys."

"Like this?" asked Mr. Gordon, suddenly rising.
He began to whistle shrill and fast, and to dance in
time to the music. It was lively and contagious. Mrs.
Gordon and Jock began to sing the tune and the rest
clapped in time to it. So Mr. Gordon stopped whistling and gave his breath to the dancing. His right
arm was flung high above his head, his feet flew
faster and faster. The floor boards of the gallery

shook with his quick pounding feet. Karl had never seen anything like it.

"What is he doing?" Karl asked.

"The Highland Fling," answered Jock, stopping his singing a minute.

"Highland clans?" Karl asked. Jock nodded and they exchanged a glance. The Clan!

The dance ended with a wild Highland shout and Mr. Gordon sat down to a burst of applause. Even Jim was clapping. Before Mr. Gordon had caught his breath the boys were demanding, "Could you teach us? Could the Clan do it?"

"Better than I!" gasped Mr. Gordon. "Ye are younger and havna been digging postholes all day." He mopped his forehead. "Aye, I could teach it, but would they be allowed to give it?" He turned toward Mr. Zorn.

"A Scotch dance at a German picnic," chuckled Pa. "Sure, why not? I'll talk to the committee in charge about it."

"Don't tell them what it is," said Karl. "Just say some of the boys of our school want to do a dance. We'll surprise them!"

"Yes," said Ma, smiling. "I think you will."

Suddenly Jim Dark spoke. "Will we all go? Or is it private?"

Pa said, "We'll all go, of course. The German League is planning it but I don't think it is only for the members. At any rate, I am a member and you will, of course, be my guests."

"Why, thank you, Mr. Zorn!" Jim smiled suddenly; then having talked more than he generally did in a week, he rose and went into the house.

"Yon's a queer lad," said Mr. Gordon.

"Yes, but he is a good hard worker," said Pa. "He is fine with the animals. I always trust a man who is good with animals. He is straightening out."

That evening was the beginning of a long training for the Clan. Jock knew some of the steps and Karl was quick and light on his feet. They learned quickly, and after the Clan had had a few evenings of instruction from Mr. Gordon the two boys could drill the Clan in the afternoons. The boys were as enthusiastic as Karl and Jock and worked hard.

They all worried about what to wear. There was no chance of a regular kilted costume, but Ma and Mrs. Gordon made tartans of plaid gingham to be tied under the right arm and high on the left shoulder. These and their Glengarry bonnets, brave with the bluebonnet badges, would, they hoped, suggest the Scottish costume.

"I'm afraid that the bluebonnets will all be gone by the first of May," said Karl.

"Most of them will be," said Ma. She was hemming a tartan. "But there is that patch down in the hollow near the creek that always blooms late. Maybe you will be able to find eleven small sprigs for your caps." Karl hoped so, for the Clan wouldn't be properly costumed without their bluebonnet badge.

One day as school let out, Karl delayed a few minutes finishing up his work. He was the last one to go to the row of pegs where they hung their coats and hats and when he got there the pegs were empty. His Glengarry bonnet was gone! He ran outside quickly and asked each one, "Have you seen my cap?" But no one had. The Clan gathered around and each looked to be sure that he had his own cap. But any way you counted, there were eleven boys and ten caps. Karl's was gone.

" 'Tis that Bill again!" said Jock. They all looked at each other. Bill had already left. Was he still keeping up his meanness about Karl's cap? Since they all wore the caps and no one paid any attention to his teasing, he had stopped, but with Bill you could not be sure.

Mr. Adams came out and locked the school door. Karl told him that his cap was gone. The teacher smiled. "I'll ask about it in school tomorrow," he said. "Things change, don't they, Karl? Six months ago you would have been glad to lose that cap."

"Yes, sir," said Karl. "But not now. Especially not now."

Karl turned toward home, thinking, "First I wanted

a big hat because I felt big hats made brave men. Then Jock explained about Glengarry caps and when I wore the bonnet I felt like a brave chieftain. Now I haven't either." He sighed. The games would have no meaning without that cocky Scotch bonnet.

"Hey! Where are you going?" called Pee Wee. "We were going to practice in our back lot, remember? And then you said you'd tell us about a new game you'd planned."

"Oh, yes!" Karl didn't feel in the mood but the Clan did need the practice. Beau King and Niclas Piast were awfully slow at learning the steps.

They practiced long and hard. Karl forgot about his cap. He took Beau and Niclas aside and drilled them separately while Jock worked with the others. Finally Karl said, "That is enough. You do better each time. Now let's rest." They flung themselves down on the grass. After a while Tom said, "What about that game you were talking about?"

Karl sat up eagerly. "It is in *The Lady of the Lake*. There is this James Fitz James—only he is really the king—who gets lost out hunting. And a Highlander is guiding him and *he* is really Roderick Dhu, an outlaw chieftain, the king's enemy. The king doesn't know that or that all the clansmen are hiding in the heather all around him. Then the Highlander calls them and they rise up everywhere and he says,

'*These are Clan Alpine's warriors true,*
And, Saxon, I am Roderick Dhu.' "

"Whew!" breathed Pee Wee. "What did the king
do?"

"Oh, he was brave. He was all alone with his en-
emies but he backed up against a rock and said,

'*Come one, come all, this rock shall fly*
From its firm base as soon as I!'

The chieftain called off his men and led the king to his
own land and then they had a fight and the king won.
It will make a fine game."

"Whew!" said Pee Wee again. "You be Roderick,
Karl."

"No, Roderick must be a big man," said Karl.
"Tom, you're tallest. I'll be the Saxon." Karl called
his orders. "Now, the rest of you hide in the heather
—I mean the weeds, of course—and don't show your-
self until you hear Roderick's signal. Then the whole
mountain that I thought was empty will be alive
with men."

Karl and Tom drew away from the rest. This was
fun! thought Karl. His fair hair blowing into his
eyes reminded him for the first time that he didn't
have on his bonnet. Suddenly he knew that it didn't
matter. He felt just as bold and valiant. And the Clan
followed his leadership as they had always done in
the games. He felt free and powerful. What you

wore didn't make any difference. Hats didn't matter —big or little, old or new. It was himself—what he thought and did and said were what mattered.

The cap did not turn up the next day at school. No one had seen it. There wasn't anywhere to look, for the pegs for hats and wraps were in plain view. There were even fewer things on the pegs today, for the morning was warm and there were no coats and shawls. Bill was absent. "I wager he kens something aboot it," Jock whispered fiercely.

This was Friday. The boys worked hard on their Highland Fling that afternoon. Saturday afternoon Mr. Gordon worked with them and said he was sure they would give a good performance when the time came.

Ma said that night, "Karlchen, I could make you a cap, I think. There is a little plaid left over from the tartans."

Karl gave her a quick smile. "It is funny, but I don't want any other cap. Maybe we will find mine yet. But if we don't, I don't want any other. It just wouldn't be the same."

"I see," said Ma and dropped the idea of a substitute.

Monday Bill shambled into school late. He said he had been working in Brenham. Mr. Adams nodded his acceptance of the excuse. The children thought it sounded pretty grown-up when your work kept you from school.

The Clan were all in the schoolyard, making plans that afternoon, when Bill came out of the school door. He was swaggering more than usual. He wore a Glengarry bonnet!

Jock saw him first. "Karl's bonnet!" he screamed.

"You thief!" shrilled Pee Wee.

"Give it back!" ordered Tom.

Eleven boys rushed toward Bill, who stood and stared with open mouth—could it be in surprise?

Karl was in the lead. As he ran he looked at the jaunty cap with its crisp creases. "Stop!" he yelled. "Stop! That's not my cap! That's a brand new one. Mine's old now."

The Clan stopped and looked at the cap. "You're right," said Jock. " 'Tis a new one. And by what right do you wear a Scottish bonnet?" he demanded belligerently.

Bill was still looking astonished. "What's the row?" he asked. "Can't a guy buy a cap without everybody going crazy?"

"Bill wasn't here Friday," Karl reminded the Clan. "Bill, my cap disappeared last week and we thought you had it."

"Me take your cap? That's *good!* I bought this cap myself. I've got lots of money." And Bill jingled coins in his pocket.

"How did you get Mr. Cartwright to sell you a cap?" Karl didn't sound mad, only curious, and Bill answered him calmly.

"I told him that I am joining the Clan."

Suddenly Karl *was* mad, very mad. The nerve, the *nerve* of Bill! "You can't walk up and say you are joining the Clan! *We* decide that, not you! You can't! You can't! Just by buying a bonnet. Not after all you have done!"

"That you canna!" cried Jock. "Jeering at Karl's cap and at ours, too, and then thinking you can be a member because *you* say so! You'd try to boss the whole Clan."

"I would not," growled Bill. "You let Tom in."

"But he promised to obey the rules, and he has," put in Pee Wee.

"Well, I could too," Bill said.

"The Clan, it is so peaceful now," said Ramon. "You would make, maybe, trouble."

"No, I wouldn't," said Bill, mildly for him. Then he just stood and waited. Karl's anger faded a little. To see the big, powerful, blustering boy just waiting to hear the verdict of the Clan seemed somehow out of place. Karl was disturbed. He didn't want to be mean, but he couldn't forget all his miserable days —all due to Bill.

"Are you sure you want to join? You made so much fun of my cap," he said.

"I still think it is queer," admitted Bill, taking off his cap and looking at it. "But I'll wear it to be one of the gang."

Pee Wee said wonderingly, "I believe he means it."

Karl saw that they could not decide here on the school grounds. "We'll go up to the chalk bank for a meeting. You wait down by the creek, Bill. The Clan must decide, not you." He thought it would be kinder not to have all the argument in front of Bill.

At the cave the argument was wild. Tom was all for admitting Bill; he had missed him. Pee Wee held to the idea that Bill meant what he said and would behave himself. Ramon was always for the underdog and, after his one protest, was on Bill's side. Jock was firmly against him. The others varied from mild doubts to open antagonism. Karl didn't know what to think. Bill in Clan Texas—a friend! But perhaps if he were inside he would make less trouble than outside, working against them. And he kept seeing Bill standing there against them all, wanting to join but too proud to plead. He had an idea.

"We might take him on trial," he suggested, "take him for a month—see if he fits in. If he behaves himself that long we'll know he means it. What do you think?"

"That would be after the picnic," said Jock, figuring. "We need an even number for the dance."

Karl grinned. "He bought the last cap. You ought to be for him."

Jock said stoutly, "I'll not be bought," but he laughed. "Well, let's take a vote."

On these terms the Clan decided to take Bill on trial. Pee Wee ran down the hill to tell him.

Now they told Bill all the plans for the picnic and the Clan's dance. "Do you think you can learn in the short time we have?" asked Karl. Bill agreed to try and they started their practicing. The big awkward boy was clumsy at it, but he plugged away at it seriously. Bill was trying hard to fit in.

Jock watched him and at last said, "Come over tonight and perhaps my dad can help you."

Karl and Jock went home together in the dusk. "It has been a very strange day," said Karl.

"Aye," said Jock. Then he added, "But Bill still thinks the bonnet is silly." That was the hardest thing of all for Jock to forgive.

· TEN ·

At last it was the first of May and the Zorn household were on their way to the grove near Brenham where the picnic would be held. Ma and Mrs. Gordon, their fresh, light, cotton dresses covered carefully with a lap-robe, sat on the seat of the wagon beside Mr. Gordon, who was driving. Pa and Jim and the boys sat on boxes and boards in the back of the wagon. Around their feet were crowded the lunch baskets, crammed full of good things and covered with red-checked tablecloths. In another basket were the Clan tartans, neatly folded and also covered with a checked cloth so that no one would see them before the dances. The boys had kept their secret well and did not want anyone to know about their costumes before they appeared on the stage.

As they neared town, young men and women on horseback and people in light buggies passed them. From each side road that turned into the main road came other wagons. Everyone wore his best clothes and waved and called to each other. Ma said over her shoulder, "It's like going to camp meeting, isn't it?"

"Camp meeting without the meeting," added Karl. That was what he had wished for last year.

"Different in other ways, too," said Pa. "We go with a wagon full today."

"Different in many ways," thought Karl. Last summer he had been so lonely; now he had Jock with him and today he would be with the Clan. Even Bill was his friend now.

He said to Jock, "Bill has been pretty good, hasn't he?"

"Most of the time," grinned Jock. "Sometimes he's tried to run things but the Clan has kept him in his place. And he will be all right in the dance."

"On the back row," agreed Karl. Bill hadn't liked practicing and was terribly clumsy at it but had worked hard. "And he thought of getting Mr. Adams to play for our dance," Karl added. The music had been a big problem. Mr. Cartwright, taken into their secret, had found the music for the Highland Fling among his books. But they had not wanted to ask the little German band to learn the piece for them. Then Bill had thought of Mr. Adams' violin and he had agreed to play for them. This had solved their last problem.

Everyone was in a holiday mood. Ma and Mrs. Gordon talked happily together on the front seat and the boys chatted in back. Pa was humming contentedly. Jim sat relaxed, smoking a homemade cigarette. When he finished he threw the lighted end to the roadside. Pa said gravely, "Never do that, Jim, even in spring when the grass is green. Fires in the country can be serious things."

Jim nodded, "Yes, sir." Even Jim was in a pleasant mood.

They had started early from the farm but it was mid-morning when they reached the picnic grounds and unloaded. The boys began at once to explore. "It seems like *everybody* is here," said Karl. "The doctor, the mayor, all the school and people we haven't seen since last year."

"And the ones who came over on the *Mississippi*," added Jock. "I didna think I would like tae see them, but I do."

"They look better and happier," said Karl. Sometimes it was hard to tell which were old-time Texans and which were the newcomers. Instead of the dark, heavy clothes they had been wearing, the immigrants today wore cotton dresses or shirts and cotton trousers like everyone else. Karl saw the little old lady, still knitting, but talking happily to some of the Brenham women. The two little "scared" girls dashed by in a wild game of tag. Even some of the men who had caused trouble were wandering around, smoking and talking and relaxed.

Everyone was called together by the band starting to play. The singing groups sang and the mayor made

a speech. He welcomed everyone and said he hoped
that this Mayday picnic would be such a success that
it would be a yearly event. Everyone clapped. But
this was only the preliminary to the real event of the
day. The baskets and boxes piled on the long tables
under the trees were more interesting than anything
a speaker could say. Now the women began unpack-
ing and proudly displaying their handiwork. Some of
the men started a fire for the big coffeepots. The
children hovered around, sniffing happily.

The long tables were made of boards laid across
saw-horses and were spread with the checked tablecloths from the baskets. Down their length was ar-
rayed the food that Ma and the other women had
worked for days preparing. As he sat down, Karl's
mouth watered. There were platters piled high with
fried chicken, crisp and golden. There was herring
salad, prepared with potatoes and beets and apples,
and Kartoffel Salat, the German potato salad, made
with bacon and vinegar. And there were thick, crusty
sandwiches of ham on pumpernickel bread. And the
pickles: dill-gherkins, and pickled onions and spiced
peaches and watermelon rind preserves. And finest
of all were the desserts: pies and cakes, Mrs. Gordon's
Scotch shortbread, Ma's caraway seed cookies and
Mrs. Schmidt's pannkuchen, doughnuts filled with
plum jam. There was coffee with yellow cream, or

lemonade, which the children drank, or beer from a keg for the menfolks.

Karl looked at the array helplessly. Even if he took only a bite of each he would be full, and everything looked so good that he wanted a lot of each. He started in manfully and it was surprising how much he was able to put away. But everyone else was doing the same, laughing and talking and eating with gusto.

While they were eating a woman across the table said to Ma, "Mrs. Zorn, was it not your son who lost his cap at school?"

"Why, yes," said Ma. Karl and Jock and the members of the Clan who were at the table pricked up their ears.

"Well, we found it this morning when we were getting out wraps to bring with us. It was inside my little girl's coat. She must have hung it over the cap and then brought it home folded. Go get it, Susan, it is in the buggy with our things."

When she gave the Glengarry bonnet to him, Karl put it on. It was good to feel it back in its proper place. Jock and the other Clan members clustered around him. "It looks fine," said Pee Wee.

"Now our chief is properly bonneted," put in Jock.

They all seemed more excited about its return than Karl was himself. "I'm glad it came back before the program," he said, then added, wonderingly, to Ma, "It ought to make me feel more excited and different, having it back, but it doesn't."

"You are growing up, Karlchen," said Ma, smiling a little sadly.

After lunch the women cleared the tables, chattering happily. The men wandered around, smoking and talking. The Clan and some of the other children started a game of hide-and-seek. There were many good places to hide, trees and clumps of bushes, the shrubbery down by the little creek, the pavilion where the dancing would be, later in the afternoon. Karl found a good place to hide, in a thick clump of sumac bushes near the steps of the pavilion. They led to the entrance to the stage. A group of men, sitting on the steps, added to the security of the hiding place. As Karl crouched down he realized that they were the men who had been the troublemakers the day when the immigrants arrived. Owens was there and Jim Dark, puffing on another cigarette.

Karl thought, "I hope they have gotten over their trouble-making." He was pleased to hear Jim say, "Well, Mr. Zorn is a prince. He treats me right. He is going to keep me on at regular pay after my passage is paid. Says I am to have entire charge of the animals." Jim saying all that! And sounding so contented!

Another man said, "I have a chance to work a farm

on shares. It will be a good place for my children."

Then Karl heard Owens' emphatic voice. "I am going farther west," he announced. "Fellow where I work has a ranch beyond the Pecos, *real* Texas. This place is too tame."

All the men laughed. "You thought it was a wilderness a few months ago," said another voice. "I'm staying right here. I like these people, hardworking but friendly. We have never been so well off."

"Why," thought Karl, "they are getting to be Texans already." He had been so interested that he forgot he was hiding. Then he heard Pee Wee, who was "it," shout shrilly, "The rest of you can come in free!" and heard the German band tuning up inside the dancehall, so he ran around the building toward the front entrance, where everyone was crowding into the building. Jock called to him from the crowd, "Wait for me," and they went on together.

Near the door they came up to Pa and Mr. Cartwright and the mayor, looking anxiously at the group of men led by Owens.

"I don't like to see that bunch together," said the mayor. "It might mean trouble."

"We'll keep an eye on them," promised Pa easily. "They look quiet enough, but you can't tell."

Mr. Cartwright said, "I think they are settling down. I have visited them where they work and they seem to be giving satisfaction. They may just enjoy being together again."

Karl interrupted eagerly, "Oh, yes, sir, they are! I heard them talking and they were just as nice and peaceful. And, Pa, Jim said you were a prince!"

"A prince, eh?" Pa chuckled. "He never told *me* that." They all went into the dancehall.

The dance pavilion looked festive with flags and bunting. The German band up on the small stage was starting a gay waltz. Soon everyone was dancing: the young couples, the children, the parents and even some of the grandparents, stepping to the music they had known in Germany, in Bohemia, in Poland or at other dances like this in other parts of this country. The big horn made a constant oom-pah, oom-pah, that marked the rhythm of the fast-moving feet.

Karl asked Ma for the first polka. He stumbled through the frisky dance, but Ma did it as deftly as she would turn a seam or scour the floor. She lifted her full, sprigged calico skirts and her little feet flew. At the end Karl was breathless but Ma just settled her skirts and there she was, as dainty and composed as ever, not one flaxen hair out of place.

"That was fine, Karlchen," she said as Pa came toward them. "Pa wants this next waltz. Don't dance too much. You want to be fresh for your Clan dance."

Karl nodded and wandered off to a bench. He

watched proudly as Pa swung Ma out onto the floor. There was Mr. Cartwright, as erect and soldierly as ever, dancing with Mrs. Gordon, and Mr. Gordon prancing off with a fat German grandmother, like a squirrel frisking around a mountain. Jock was trying to steer Katy Riley around, and the two little girls who used to be so timid were hopping around together and getting in everybody's way. Some of the Clan were dancing and some, like Karl, were watching. The benches had a scattering of spectators: women with babies, old people who were not able to keep the fast pace and others resting between dances.

Bill came and sat down by Karl. "I can't see why anyone dances for *fun*," he said. "It is hard work for me."

Karl grinned, "But you are all right when you practice," he said encouragingly.

At the end of the dance Jock came up to them. "We didna get the basket with the tartans in it," he said anxiously. "And it's just like the ither lunch baskets. Should we not go look for it?"

"That's right," agreed Karl. "Come on, Bill, let's find them. We want to be ready."

The three boys left the dancehall and went to the tables where the women had left the baskets. They peeped under many red-checked tablecloths but saw only scraps or empty dishes. They found a pail half full of Ma's cookies. Karl picked it up. "Let's take these with us. Maybe the basket is still in the wagon," and, nibbling cookies as if they had not eaten before today, they went over to where the wagons stood with the shafts down while the horses grazed in the field beyond. There they found the basket and started with it toward the pavilion.

"Let's put it by the steps by the stage door," said Karl. "Then we will have it when we need it. Our dance will be just after the costume dance." So the boys turned toward that end of the building.

All three boys saw it at once—the blaze leaping up around the steps and the smoke pouring forth. Fire! They started to run toward it. They must do something at once! All those people inside! Someone might get hurt! Then Karl thought of something else—two thoughts flashing quickly through his mind as he ran. "Jock," he panted. "Get the Clan! Don't tell anyone else!"

"Aye," said Jock. "And I'll not tell." And he turned and ran toward the front door of the pavilion.

"Come on," said Karl to Bill. "The creek!" He grabbed the tablecloth from the basket and ran toward the water. Bill, who was carrying the pail of cookies, dumped them on the ground and followed with the empty pail.

Water on the cloth, in the pail, on the fire! Back

for more, dipping, running, pouring, beating! The two dashed back and forth, sometimes seeming to conquer the flame, only to see it break out in another place.

"Why not tell everyone?" asked Bill, breathless. "This is bad!"

"Might cause panic," Karl panted, as he dipped the tablecloth. "And those immigrants were sitting here —people might blame them—didn't do it on purpose!" He was running as he talked. Now he beat the flames with the cloth. "Might have made trouble. The Clan can manage," and he dashed back toward the creek.

"Yeah," said Bill. He saw a flame high against the door frame, and reaching with his cap, he just managed to beat it out. Another! He was stretching and reaching and beating when Jock and the rest of the Clan dashed up. On the way they had grabbed some blankets people had been sitting on and the big lemonade pail.

It was easier after that with twelve boys working, beating with the blankets, smothering fugitive flames, splashing water. They soon had the fire under control. A few more buckets of water sloshed on, a few minutes of watching to be sure there was no smoldering bit unnoticed and then there was only the blackened door and steps, the acrid odor and sooty water where the fire had been. The boys flung themselves on the grass.

Mr. Cartwright appeared, walking quickly and looking anxious. A glance told him everything that had happened. "A fire! Those wretched trouble-makers!"

"No, sir," said Karl. "Somebody dropped a cigarette. Not on purpose. I was afraid people would think that."

"Sae we put it out ourselves," added Jock.

"Why didn't you call some of the men?" asked Mr. Cartwright. "Was it because you wanted all the credit to go to the Clan?"

"Oh, no!" cried all the boys, and Jock added, "We didna want people frightened."

"Or stirred up and angry at the immigrants," said Karl earnestly. "It might have made trouble, a fight, maybe. And it was not a large fire. The Clan could manage it."

"Yes, I see," agreed Mr. Cartwright. "Maybe you were right."

"How did you know, sir?" asked Pee Wee. "Did we make a lot of noise?"

"No, you couldn't hear a thing with all the noise inside," said Mr. Cartwright. "I saw Jock gather the Clan and then they did not return. I thought I smelled smoke, thought it might be the picnic fires and came out to see what was happening."

He looked at the blackened entrance. "I don't know how to thank you for acting so quickly and quietly. You have given these men their chance and given me a chance, too. I want to bring over more of these people. If there had been any more trouble with this first lot no one would have wanted them. And if their neighbors had turned against them, these men might have gone back to their old discontent and rebellion. I will explain to everyone later so they will understand. Thank you all!"

He looked at them earnestly, then he smiled at the black, grimy faces before him.

"You certainly look like the Fire Brigade! What happened to your cap, Bill?"

Bill was turning the cap slowly in his hands. It was smoke-stained and out of shape and the ribbons were burned completely off.

"Bill was the best fire-fighter of all," said Karl. "He could carry more water than we could. He beat the flames with his cap. He could reach where we couldn't."

"That cap is gone," said Pee Wee. "What will you do about the Highland fling?"

"Stay out of it," said Bill. "I'd like to."

"No," said Karl. "Take my cap. I don't mind."

Bill smoothed out his sooty cap and put it defiantly on his head. His voice, when he spoke, had the old jeering note. "That sissy cap!" he drawled. "I wouldn't wear it. I like my own, it hasn't any silly ribbons!"

The Clan looked at him a minute and then roared. Bill was joking!

"Good old Bill!" cried Tom, thumping him on the back.

"Bill's a regular Clansman, now," shrilled Pee Wee.

"Worthy of the bonnet, dinna you think?" Jock asked of Karl. Karl nodded.

"Yes, yes!" yelled all the Clan.

"If you still expect to do your dance," said Mr. Cartwright, "I suggest that you go down to the creek and clean up." He reached in his pocket and drew out an immaculate handkerchief and a comb, which he handed to them. "It won't be long until the program dances begin."

"The tartans, where are they?" said Karl. But they were safe, back where he had dropped the basket—all fresh and folded as Ma had packed them. And the little sprays of blue-bonnets were still fresh in damp paper.

What brushing of clothes, what washing of hot, blackened faces and grimy hands, drying them on Mr. Cartwright's handkerchief! What passing of Mr. Cartwright's comb from one boy to another! Then the tartans were tied under the right arm and high on the left shoulder and the Glengarry bonnets were brushed and carefully creased and adorned with their blue-bonnet crests, as the music and stomping of the folk dances sounded inside the hall.

Mr. Adams put his head out the door, not noticing the blackened panels or the sooty steps in his hurry. "All ready, out there?" he called.

"Just about," answered Mr. Cartwright.

"Line up," said Karl. "Put on your bonnets."

Twelve Glengarry bonnets were proudly adjusted on twelve damp heads. The first quick strains of the Highland Fling shrilled from Mr. Adams' violin.

"Forward, men!" commanded the chieftain of Clan Texas and led his clansmen up the blackened steps and onto the stage.